THE SHORT CAUTION

THE SHORT CAUTION

GARY COYNE

ORION

First published in Great Britain in 1994 by Orion
An imprint of Orion Books Ltd
Orion House, 5 Upper St Martin's Lane,
London WC2H 9EA

A CIP catalogue record for this book is
available from the British Library

ISBN 1 85797 562 6

Typeset by Deltatype Ltd, Ellesmere Port, Cheshire
Printed in Great Britain by Butler & Tanner, Frome and London

For Jayne and Antonia

CHAPTER 1

I was rudely awakened from my miserable slumber by the heat of the morning sun on my less than attractive face. This June heatwave had pushed even the latest sex scandals out of the tabloid headlines. The rays of bright light filtering through the grubby Venetian blinds seemed to catch the dust particles in the air like prisoners in a searchlight. The dust had accumulated to hazardous levels since the office had last been cleaned, which was around the time Glenn Miller went missing.

I'd fallen asleep at my desk again. Whenever I'm stupid enough to have a drink with my partner, Ralph Grice, I end up in this sorry state. The blotter was damp from my dribble, and my head throbbed like the Tardis before take-off. An empty bottle of Ralph's favourite cheap and nasty blended whisky stood next to the phone. One of his carelessly discarded Woodbines had burned a black mark into the desk top. Beer cans were strewn around the floor. All in all, the place looked more like a squat than a professional office.

My name's Jack Mayo and, together with Ralph, we form *Mayo & Grice, Private Detectives*. Our windows and doors are marked in the time-honoured fashion, in gold paint, announcing ourselves and our profession to the world.

I got to my feet, scratched my backside, and walked

across to the windows. It was a little after ten o'clock on a Saturday morning. Through the film of dirt on the window I could make out the heavy traffic on the Stratford Road and the shoppers, mostly Asian, going about their business. Ralph, meanwhile, was conspicuous by his absence.

We're both ex-cops. The first time I met Ralph was on a Sunday evening back in early February, 1981. We were two new recruits in a group of about fifty who had turned up, invited, at the police training school at Ryton-on-Dunsmore, just outside Coventry. As I walked into the main hall to find out which class I would be in, Ralph was being given the first of the many bollockings he would receive over the next ten weeks. This particular chewing-out came as a result of Ralph smoking, despite the clear No Smoking signs, smelling like a pub drip-tray and generally looking like a bag of shit.

Most would-be cops had arrived with short hair, wearing suits and having just enough nous to realise that liberal use of the word 'sir' would be to their advantage.

Ralph arrived in dirty jeans, a black leather jacket and filthy training shoes. His hair was unkempt and his five o'clock shadow had developed into a seven o'clock shadow. He did not further endear himself to the training sergeants by addressing them as 'pal'.

It was my ill luck to find myself in the same class as Ralph. Furthermore, my room in the residential block was next to his. Later, we would be posted to the same shift at the same police station. Having joined West Midlands Police together, we left at different times and for different reasons. I was given a medical pension at the end of ten years' service, after I developed serious problems with my right knee. Ralph was sacked for something he didn't do: he *didn't* hold his temper when the Chief Inspector criticised an arrest he'd made, and Ralph apparently felt obliged to break his cheekbone with a classic right hook. Ralph dismissed it, later, as a 'lucky shot'. No charges were brought against him. It was felt, by the hierarchy, that further bad press for West Midlands Police was something to be avoided. The incident was swept under the carpet and Ralph, after a brief disciplinary hearing, was swept out of the job.

I left with a modest pay-off and a small pension. I used some of the cash to set up this business and it's been going for a year or so now. As fate would have it, three months ago I met Ralph in a pub and, after one scotch too many, was daft enough to make him a partner in my fledgling enterprise. Overnight, *Jack Mayo, Private Detective* became *Mayo & Grice, Private Detectives*. I had to fight hard to prevent it becoming *Grice & Mayo*. I'd plucked Ralph from the dole queues, where he spent his days, and the nightclubs, where he moonlighted in the evenings as a bouncer. So far he had proved to be an asset, in the same way an electic blanket is an asset to somebody sleeping in a doorway. *Mayo & Grice*, I should point out, is a non-profitmaking organisation. We don't mean to be, we just are.

This dump I laughingly call an office is let to me by an Asian friend, Mr Ahmed, at a poppadum rent. Ahmed owns the whole block, a three-storey affair with absolutely no architectural merit. Birmingham City Council would have demolished the place by now if there had been. Ralph and I occupy the top floor. There's the office itself and a small bedsit across the landing, where Ralph lives, as well as a bathroom. If our office looks like a tip, you should see inside Ralph's bedsitter. I live out in Chasetown, Staffordshire, with my wife and two kids. Wife, kids, mortgage, job . . . the 'full catastrophe' as Zorba The Greek put it. It's a round trip every day of more than thirty miles, but it's worth it to be so far from Ralph.

Directly beneath our office is an Asian private-hire taxi firm, *Black & Blue Taxis*, so-called because the drivers are frequently beaten up. On the ground floor is *Mick's Tattoo Parlour*. The area is Sparkbrook, where the Stratford Road begins to close in on the city centre. Here, every other shop you see sells second-hand goods – which accounts for the tatty furniture in my office. When you walk into *Mayo & Grice*, you could be forgiven for thinking you were in Churchill's War Rooms. Our colour scheme is drab olive and white with a hint of soot. The green revolving light from the taxi firm, located above their window and therefore below ours, lights up our office at night like a pub disco.

Next door is *Srinegar Mo's Balti House*, where Ralph spends most nights dipping his naan bread. Whether he dips before or after he's consumed his statutory twelve pints of bitter is entirely dependent on his mood. Mohammed, the owner, gives him a generous discount and, in return, Ralph ejects any patrons who get on Mohammed's nerves – or, alternatively, on Ralph's. Incidentally, the Balti House is unlicensed so, if you decide to visit, take a bottle. Naturally, the cooking smells permeate the whole block.

Further down the street towards town is a pawnbroker, whose sign possesses two more balls than Hitler, a bookie's and a pigsty of a late-night café called the Capri, run by a malodorous chap known as Cheesy Vic.

In the other direction, we are next door to *Diane's Sauna & Massage*, which is just a misspelling of 'brothel'. Diane offers hand relief for a tenner. My guess is that Ralph is, at this very moment, in with Diane or one of her girls having his hand relieved. Ralph gets a 'police discount' there, as well.

It was at this point that I noticed the smell in the office. Clearly, it wasn't the waft of Mohammed's spices being skilfully blended. I recognised the odour and moved quickly to shut the toilet door. Ralph's stomach and bowels are a class double-act, capable of turning the most innocuous meal into foul-smelling toxic waste. You can imagine, then,

4

what occurs after he's consumed his 'Special Meat Balti' and a gallon and a half of ale. We keep a canary in a cage nearby.

I opened a window and looked outside. Another hot, sweaty day. This used to be an Irish district. Now they've moved further down the Stratford Road to Hall Green and Asians have taken their place. The buildings are moribund but the community continues to thrive. We've got Asian banks, saree shops, corner grocers open almost round the clock, second-hand car retailers with more coloured bunting than you'd find on Blackpool's Golden Mile, and Asian-run video stores with the latest hot-releases from The Punjab.

As I breathed in the welcome carbon monoxide, I saw a little silver Mini drive up onto the wide pavement in front of the building and park adjacent to one of those No Waiting At Any Time posts. A young woman with dyed blonde hair and a shapely figure got out and looked up at our window. She gave a little smile and headed towards the communal entrance downstairs and out of my sight. I knew she would have to step over the prostrate body of Claude, the black dosser who lives out of a cardboard box in the doorway. Judging from the smell, his box is *en-suite*.

I wasn't expecting a customer that morning. If I'm honest, I wasn't expecting a customer that month. The clip-clopping of the young woman's shoes could be heard coming up the wooden stairs, then my office door opened and the girl with dyed blonde hair walked in. She was twitching her nostrils.

'It's the drains,' I explained.

'Oh.' She smiled, showing even white teeth. She was wearing a white cotton flying suit and white court shoes. Her skin was pale but it looked healthy. Her blonde hair had no more black roots than Alex Haley. She was tall and attractive, with full pouting lips and blue eyes. Ralph would

5

describe her, later, as having 'a fellatial face'. Thanks, Ralph. Her eyes were puffy, like she'd been crying, or not getting enough sleep, or both. The blonde hair was hanging down over her left eye and she habitually brushed it back. I noticed, as ex-cops are prone to do, that she was bra-less, her suit top being unbuttoned nearly to the waist.

'Mr Mayo?' she said, in a husky voice.

'That's me,' I replied, trying hard not to stare at her cleavage. I guided her to a chair and motioned her to sit down. She did so, placing her handbag on the floor and crossing her legs. The suit trousers ended just below the knee, showing off two shapely calves.

'How can I help you?' I said, trying to hold in my stomach and suddenly aware that I hadn't washed, shaved or cleaned my teeth. Now I knew how Ralph felt, every day.

'I want to hire you, Mr Mayo. You were recommended to me by a mutual friend.'

'I'm not certain I have any friends, Miss . . . ?'

'Mrs Johnson – Theresa Johnson. Everyone calls me Tess, though.'

I spotted the ring on her third finger, left hand. The way she was sitting had caused her top to fall open and she was revealing rather more of her right breast than I'm sure she had intended. I gave it my undivided attention.

'I live over in Burntwood, Mr Mayo.'

'Call me Jack,' I said.

'I was told you used to be a policeman, a detective, in Birmingham. Is that right?'

'Yeah – and so was my partner, Mr Grice. Part of the thin blue line. Can I offer you a cup of coffee, Tess?'

'Please. Black, no sugar.'

I walked across to the refreshment facility – a stained enamel tray supporting a fine selection of dirty, chipped mugs, all of which carried an advert for a local boarding-up company. I found two mugs which were slightly less disgusting than the rest and tipped their dregs into a third mug, in which a bluebottle was thrashing about, and switched on the kettle. Since the heat had turned the milk rancid, I decided to take my coffee black, too.

'Why did you leave the police, Jack?' Tess asked.

'I retired on a medical pension, with a dicky knee. Now I walk like a man who's been bowled LBW without shinpads, especially in cold weather.'

'What about Mr Grice – why did he leave?'

'A similar story. He hurt his, er, hand. Now,' I said, quickly changing the subject, 'why exactly do you want to hire us?'

'My husband is in Winson Green Prison, Jack, on remand awaiting trial for a murder he didn't commit. The police are convinced he did. I want you to find the real killer because it's the only sure way of getting my husband released.'

I poured boiling water over the cheap and nasty chicory-based imitation coffee that Ralph had purchased. 'Cheap and nasty' are bywords for Ralph. They are probably written in Latin on his family's coat of arms. (I shudder to think what else may be depicted there.) I stirred the mixture and took a mug across to Mrs Johnson.

'If you have evidence that your husband didn't commit the murder, Tess, you should go to the police with it. They work for free.' Damn – I was talking myself out of a job.

'I don't have any evidence – just a gut feeling.'

Right on cue after those two last words, the door opened and Ralph walked in. He looked like he'd slept in a builder's skip. His suit was creased, his tie crooked, his hair uncombed and, worst of all, his flies were undone.

'This is Mr Grice,' I apologised.

'Pleased to meet you,' Tess said, standing up.

'Ralph, this is Mrs Johnson,' I told him.

'Hello, duck,' Ralph said. He called everybody 'duck' – when he wasn't calling them 'pal'. I wondered whether he'd shake her hand or grab her breasts. Luckily, he held out a huge sweaty hand. Mrs Johnson shook it, wiped her palm on her thigh, and sat back down.

'Mrs Johnson's husband is in the Green, awaiting trial for murder, Ralph. She wants us to find the real killer.' I put it in a nutshell for Grice, who had moved across to the general environment of the kettle. I cringed as he emptied the dregs from another mug out of the open window and I hoped he hadn't soaked a passerby. Again.

'Look, Tess, it's only natural for you to think your husband is innocent. Nobody likes to think a close relative is capable of any crime, let alone murder.' I took a sip of coffee and did my best not to retch.

'I see.' Tess began to get up. 'It was obviously a mistake to come here. I thought ex-cops would be the right people to help me: I guess I was wrong. So much for the recommendations.'

'Sit down,' I said. 'I didn't say we were unwilling to help, I was just trying to be realistic. There's been a murder so the police set up an incident room. Fifty or more detectives work round the clock to solve the crime and your old man is charged. I just don't want to get your hopes up or waste your money.'

Ralph came and sat on the edge of the desk, to the side of Tess, a mug of coffee in his hand. His fly gaped open and I noticed he was wearing odd socks. He's a real class act, Ralph. Third, that is.

'So you'll take the job, Mr Mayo? I'll pay the proper rates.'

'Of course. Now I think you'd better tell us about the murder your husband is supposed to have committed.'

Tess took a gulp of coffee, as if to steady her resolve, and brushed the hair out of her eyes.

'Paul, my husband, is an instructor at the Amazon Gym in Lichfield. The dead girl is, or rather *was*, an aerobics teacher at the same place. A few days ago she was found dead in her car at Chasewater. There was a single stab wound to her chest and her clothes had been torn off.'

'Had she been raped or sexually assaulted?' Ralph asked. He always likes to hear the exact details – the grosser the better.

'No. Police think the killer was disturbed by some boys who arrived early for a day's fishing. It was the boys who found the body – which, I'm told, accounts for the fact that maggots were present on a corpse which had only been dead for a matter of a few minutes or seconds. One of the boys dropped his maggots, those little coloured ones.'

I tried to imagine the look on the officers' faces when they found a corpse covered in designer maggots.

Tess continued. 'This happened in the early hours of last Tuesday. On Thursday morning, Paul and I were in bed at home when the door got kicked in and half a dozen policemen piled into our bedroom. Paul was dragged out of bed, naked. So was I. Then he was told he was under arrest on suspicion of murdering Michelle Rosa, the dead girl, and told to get dressed. They searched the house and took away some of his clothing and other things.'

'Were you still naked, by now?' Ralph asked what was, I suppose, for him a crucial question.

'No. I wrapped a sheet round me. Paul was taken away to Lichfield Police Station. I got dressed and went across there, but they wouldn't let me see him. Then, hours later, while I was still sat at the station, I was told Paul had been charged with murder and would be appearing before Lichfield Magistrates the following morning, which was yesterday, Friday.'

'Who's Paul's mouthpiece – sorry, his solicitor?' I asked. Police jargon dies hard.

'Eddie English. He's based in Lichfield. Paul's employer arranged it.'

9

'Do you know what evidence the police have against Paul?'

'Eddie said something about them finding the murder weapon in his locker at the gym, plus the fact that Paul had no alibi on the night and morning of the murder.'

'Where were you?' I asked.

'In Birmingham. I'd been to a friend's hen party and stayed the night at my mother's house in Edgbaston. Paul's only alibi is that he was in bed asleep – which isn't much of an alibi without a witness.'

'I'll need to go and see English to get the full SP. Is there anything else you can tell me, Tess?' I gave up on the coffee.

'Well, yes. The police seem to be making this out to be a sex attack that was interrupted. The point is, Michelle had worked at the gym for just a fortnight. Paul told me that she had made a play for him.'

'What do you mean, exactly?' I asked.

'Paul's very attractive, Jack. He's a bodybuilder and obviously very muscular, fit, tanned and a real magnet for the girls at the gym. He takes it all in his stride but he made a point of telling me about Michelle.'

'What happened?'

'Gym finished one evening at about ten o'clock, and Paul went for a shower. Next thing, Michelle's in there alongside him, nude and pawing his body. Paul said he got out and told her straight that it just wasn't on, that he was married and so on. If that was the case, why launch a sex attack on her and kill her? It was on a plate for him anyway.'

I didn't look at Ralph's face in case he was thinking what I was thinking. I mean, any man sharing a shower with an aerobics teacher wouldn't suddenly get a bad case of morals, would he?

'Okay,' I said. 'I charge fifty pounds a day plus expenses. Obviously you double that if you want Mr Grice involved.'

My rates are very reasonable. In this area I couldn't attract work if I charged any more.

'I'd like you both involved, Jack.'

'Can you afford it, duck?' Ralph asked, obviously willing to discuss a deal where he could take payment in kind.

'Yes. I work as a temp but we've got our holiday cash and I'm working part-time in a pub four nights a week. I can cope, don't worry about that.'

Ralph looked disappointed.

'Paul and I have been saving up for two years to buy a small gym over in Greece. That's another reason why my husband wouldn't have killed this girl. The dream of a gym on a Greek island is too strong. Do you have a secretary, Jack?' Her sudden change of subject caught me on the hop.

'No. Our workload doesn't justify one – why?'

'I'm a temp. I thought I could work for you for a reduction in the fee.'

'Is today's date the twenty-fifth of July, 1955?' I asked.

'No,' she replied, looking puzzled.

'Good,' I said. 'Then we've established I wasn't born yesterday.'

She laughed and reached forward to pick up her handbag. Ralph, I noticed, took the opportunity to peer inside her open top. Tess moved her purse and counted out £400 in £50 notes.

'That's four days' money in advance, Jack. Here's my address and here's Eddie English's business card.'

In the spirit of trust endemic in cops, I held each note up to the light.

'Anything else you need to know, Jack?' Tess now stood up, brushing her hair from her eye again.

'Who owns the gym where Paul works? I mean, who arranged the solicitor?'

'Barry Raphael. He's more or less retired, even though he's probably no older than, oh, maybe his late forties.

Whatever he did for a living, he made a lot of money. You should see his house the other side of Lichfield. He drips wealth, Jack.'

She paused for a moment and I noticed tears welling up in her eyes. I hoped Ralph hadn't noticed but he had. He took out his hanky, which was in worse shape than the mugs, and offered it to Tess. I quickly diverted her gaze and led her towards the door.

'You will do your very best, Jack, won't you? I couldn't live without Paul.' She looked so helpless.

'I promise you we'll do everything we can to get Paul released. On Monday I'll go and see English. I'll ring you on Monday night.'

'If I'm not in, Jack, I'll be at work at the Viking pub in Chasetown. Leave a message for me there. Tell whoever answers it's for Theresa. They don't know me as Tess.' She nodded to us both and walked out of the office.

Ralph had already moved across to the window to watch Tess walk to her car. 'I could give her one, Jack,' he muttered, his back to me.

'She's a client, Ralph. You ever heard of this Barry Raphael bloke?'

'Arr. It's the same bloke you're obviously thinking of. Him and his brother Mick ran all the protection rackets in Brum throughout the sixties and seventies. He can afford to go legit now, greasy git. I never met the guy, though. Everyone up the town knows him by reputation. In the sixties it was either Barry or Mick who was screwing the missus of a very high-ranking police officer. Thinking about it, Jack, it must have been Barry since Mick prefers liitle boys.'

'What about English?' I asked Ralph, my personal fountain of knowledge of all things criminal.

'Bent brief. Actually did a stretch in the early seventies for a serious wounding. Took his fucking exams inside and eventually became a solicitor. Won the John McVicar Award for academic excellence whilst in HM Prison Sudbury. It don't surprise me he works for that arse-hole Raphael.'

'It's a sick world, Ralph. You've got to be squeaky clean to become a copper but you can become a solicitor despite having previous convictions.' I sounded like one of those guys who lecture the bored passers-by at Speaker's Corner on a Sunday morning.

'What did English do, anyway?' I enquired.

'Bludgeoned his wife with a rolling pin. He reckons it was a crime of passion. She obviously thought otherwise and pressed charges.'

Ralph picked up another of his whisky bottles and poured himself a local anaesthetic. 'I was thinking, Jack, about what Tess said.' He turned to face me, his fly still wide open.

'Go on,' I said.

'About that aerobics bird turning up stark naked in Paul's shower. How come things like that never happen to me?'

'You never shower, Ralph,' I said, trying to break the news gently to him.

CHAPTER 2

I spent Sunday relaxing at home with the wife and kids. We live in an old miner's cottage in Regent Street, Chasetown, just off the High Street. I noticed from the scrap of paper Tess had given me that she lived about a mile away, near Swan Island, Burntwood, in a typical thirties semi-detached house. I tried to figure out who our 'mutual friend' could have been, but nobody sprang to mind.

I got to the office early on Monday morning and found Claude, the tramp, lying in a pool of his own urine. There was an empty bottle of T-bird wine nearby. Upstairs, things were little better: the office stank like the Oktoberfest. I felt rough anyway, and the smell of Ralph's empties made me tetchy, and did nothing to dilute my natural cynicism. Add to that the usual Monday morning feeling and the harrowing prospect of having to inhale the same air as Eddie English, and you can see I was great company!

Gingerly, I opened the door of Ralph's bedsit. My partner lay asleep in his scratch pit. The room was in no more disarray than normal, resembling the aftermath of a particularly messy house burglary. I looked at Ralph's greasy hair. He could have been swimming in the wake of the *Exxon Valdez*. I threw a book at his head to get his attention.

He shot upright and shouted, 'What the fuck's going on?'

Ralph is bi-lingual, fluent in both English and Anglo-Saxon.

'Wakey, wakey Ralphie. Time to go and see Mr English.'

Ralph scratched his head, belched and swung two huge white legs out of bed. He was still wearing his odd socks. Standing upright, his beer belly hung over his Y-fronts like snow from a roof. Clearly deciding against a shower or a shave, Ralph took his Romanian Polyester-Viscose suit from the melamine wardrobe and threw it onto the bed. It was a large suit, Ralph being a large man. He is the sort of customer who is measured for a suit by a guy using a theodolite. The Romanian suit wasn't fashionable when he bought it, just after we met at Ryton, and it certainly wasn't fashionable now – even in Romania. The seat of the trousers was so shiny Ralph wasn't sure whether to have it dry cleaned or re-silvered.

First he put on a light blue shirt, which had the added attraction of salt-marks under the armpits, and a plain red tie in some hideous man-made material. The tie was food-stained. Ralph was a sartorial bag of shit.

'Don't feel you need to clean your teeth on my behalf,' I said.

'I don't. You ready, Jack?'

I followed Ralph outside where he got into the driver's side of his car, a pale blue Allegro with more miles on the clock than something from the Air Guatemala fleet. The tax disc had expired about the same time as Bing Crosby.

'I take it we're going in your car, then, Ralph?'

Ralph made no reply: he obviously wasn't in a talkative mood. So I got into the front passenger seat and wound the window down to allow his noxious gases a chance to escape. The thought of sharing a fifteen or twenty-mile journey with him in this heat depressed me. I switched on the car radio and listened to the inane warblings of the Radio One disc jockey. There's something not quite right about a man approaching fifty playing rave music. There's probably something strange about a thirty-seven-year-old bloke listening to it. Worse, I found myself humming.

Ralph was a Grade One police driver. We crewed a 'fast response car' together for a year before I transferred to CID. He was fast but safe. His road manners left everything to be desired, however. Now he took the middle ring road to avoid the city centre, where the council was busy pedestrianising the roads when they still hadn't found a way to pedestrianise the footpaths. The traffic was light and I found myself thinking about Ralph and his career in the police. He was a legend.

At Ryton he'd been called 'The Home Office Plant' since he'd struggled to come to terms with the discipline and sorely tested the patience and ability of the instructors. His marching was best described as useless; Ralph always looked like he was strolling out to get the Sunday papers. And his appearance was scruffy. His uniform trousers had tram-lines pressed into them, due to his ineptitude with the iron. Somehow, though, despite all this, and his habit of drinking at least ten pints a night in the training centre bar, Ralph managed to scrape through all his weekly exams. My one clear memory is of Ralph running along the corridor of the residential block, naked but for the black drawstring cotton bag used for carrying police helmets tied over his head. This became a nightly ritual until he was caught by the duty sergeant, who happened to be a policewoman from Northamptonshire. As a punishment she gave him extra duties. Rumour had it that these included a romp with her in the guard hut . . .

I was jolted from my thoughts by Ralph shouting at some old chap driving his Metro at twenty-five miles an hour on a de-restricted road. Ralph has his own selection of hand-signals, none of which are specified in the Highway Code.

We parked in Tesco's free car park in Lichfield, thus

saving about twenty pence. Ralph was still in laconic mood as we ambled down Tamworth Street and across Market Square. I looked at the statue of Dr Johnson and noted how he looked as pissed off as Ralph, leaning his head onto his fist. Ralph's a loner. His wife left him for a human being several years ago and since then, none of his relationships with women have lasted longer than a couple of hours.

Ralph's wife went off with a man she'd met doing amateur dramatics. Her new beau was older than Ralph, which hurt far more than if she had run off with a toy boy. Furthermore he was, and probably still is, a mature student. Ralph resented his income tax supporting a bloke he described as 'either a fucking slow learner or he knows how to screw the system'.

I met the man once and found him to have few likeable qualities. Even fewer than Ralph, in fact. He was in his mid-forties, but still stuck at the time of *Yellow Submarine* like he was in a time warp. Apparently he once told Ralph to 'mellow out', so Ralph kicked him in his tabs. The split with his wife led to Ralph going even further off the rails. He collected formal complaints at the rate of three or four a month, usually for the injudicious use of 'the short caution', which is police slang for a smack in the mouth. Ralph got suspended more times than Habeas Corpus. It was said that the Complaints Department at Lloyd House, Police HQ, had to open the Ralph Grice Annexe to keep pace with his caseload.

Finally, Ralph overstepped the mark. Having somehow or other kept his job by the shiny seat of his pants, he had occasion to deck a senior officer. God, I wish I'd seen it. One day, I should get his version of events – maybe today, on the way back to Birmingham.

It was twelve o'clock when we finished our big breakfasts at McDonald's and walked into the Erasmus Darwin Chambers in Bird Street. We had originally arrived at ten-thirty, but Ralph decided he needed some nosebag. The Chambers were in a splendid Georgian block which, had it been in Birmingham, would now be a subway or a multi-storey car park. Eddie English had a suite of offices on the first floor. The sign on the frosted glass door stated *Edward T. English, Solicitor & Commissioner For Oaths*. Inside, the waiting room was light and airy, well-appointed with a lush, pastel-green carpet and fitted furniture in black-stained ash and chrome. Very high-tech and rather out of keeping with the eighteenth-century building. I don't suppose Ralph noticed or cared. Several black leather and chrome chairs lined the wall, next to a glass and chrome coffee table littered with old magazines. A receptionist or secretary sat in the far corner, by the windows. She was a big woman of about forty-five who had squeezed her size twenty body into a size eighteen frock. I felt a picture of health by comparison.

'Can I help you gentlemen?' she enquired, in a rather cultured voice.

'I'm here to see Mr English,' I said, loosening my tie.

She looked the sort of woman who sat you on her lap to take dictation. Ralph was slumped in a chair looking at a three-year-old copy of *Homes & Gardens*. Maybe he was thinking of giving his bedsit the Shugborough look.

'Do you have an appointment?'

'No, but I'm sure he'll see us. It's about the murder case – Michelle Rosa, you know?'

'Take a seat. I'll see how busy he is. What names shall I say, Mr . . . ?'

'Mayo. Mayo and Grice. We're private detectives, hired by Mrs Johnson, the wife of English's client, Paul Johnson. You got all that?' I said.

The secretary knocked on a door and disappeared inside an office. Moments later she came out and pulled the door to behind her.

'I'm afraid Mr English has a full diary for the rest of today. However, he will be pleased to see you, by appointment, before the end of the week.' I could smell her cheap perfume as she wafted back to her desk.

Ralph bounded over to her. Before she got the chance to reposition her shapeless derrière, he'd pulled her telephone lead from the wall.

'No more calls, fat bird. We're gonna be busy in there.' Ralph was as subtle as an air raid at times. He marched over to the door of English's office and crashed in. Moments later, a chap who I took to be the solicitor's client left at the double, almost stumbling out of the room. Ralph re-appeared in the open doorway.

'Come on in, Jack. Eddie's found a gap in his diary.'

I walked into English's office, half-expecting him to be sprawled across his desk after Ralph had, maybe, dropped the nut on him. He hadn't. English stood up and walked across to shake my hand. He was a slightly-built man with a bad case of male pattern baldness. As he stood next to Ralph and pumped my hand I noticed his impeccable grooming, Savile Row to Ralph's Skid Row. His suit must have cost the best part of a grand, and I'm certain it had never been within 1500 miles of Romania.

'Jack Mayo?' he said, smiling. He looked tanned and fit. He made me want to puke.

'Yes,' I replied, 'and this is my partner, Ralph Grice.'

'Mr Grice,' English said, just nodding towards him and not risking a handshake. 'Please take a seat, gentlemen. I apologise for that little mix-up. I'm afraid my secretary got the message somewhat garbled. Would you like coffee?'

English sat back down behind his desk, which was big enough to land a Chinook on. His office was expensively fitted out in light-grey stained ash with a contrasting maroon trim. The walls were lined with bookshelves, full of heavy-looking law volumes, journals, stated cases and the ubiquitous *Stones' Justices Manuals*. Several original cartoons of a legal nature hung on the few patches of wall not covered in books. Ralph and I sat down.

'Yeah, white, no sugar for both of us,' Ralph said, and English used his desk intercom to get the fat woman up and working. The solicitor looked to me like a man who didn't sweat, even in this heat. When he smiled, his perfect white teeth made him look a little like Douglas Fairbanks, Jnr. Only the six-inch wide parting of his hair ruined the effect.

'I understand Mrs Johnson has hired you to make enquiries into the murder of Michelle Rosa.' English leaned back in his grey leather chair and clasped his hands together.

'You got that bit of the garbled message, then,' grunted Ralph.

'That's right,' I interrupted. 'She's of the opinion that her husband is entirely innocent and she hopes we can find the real killer. You're Paul Johnson's legal rep – what do you think?'

'Quite honestly, Mr Mayo, I think she's wasting her money. Having read the prosecution papers – and you should bear in mind that these are just the initial remand in custody papers – I'd reluctantly have to come to the conclusion that Johnson is guilty.'

'Based on what evidence?' I asked.

'Based on the following facts: the murder weapon was found in Johnson's locker at the gym where he works, *with his fingerprints on it*, and Michelle Rosa's panties were there as well. His T-shirt bearing the gym logo was found in the dead girl's car at the murder scene, and he was the last person to be seen with her when they left the gym together in her car that night. Then there are all the statements of various members of staff at the gym who point out Johnson's obsession with Michelle and how his lust was not reciprocated . . . Shall I go on?'

'There are certain aspects which do not tie up,' I said.

'Such as, Mr Mayo?' English sat forwards and leaned on his desk blotter, which was finished in maroon leather. Very tasteful.

'Well, supposing they left the gym together at ten-thirty. The girl's body was discovered around four in the morning by two lads out fishing. That's five and a half hours to account for, yet there's no rape, no sexual assault.'

'You've been misinformed, Mr Mayo. The police did find evidence of sexual activity – recent sexual activity – together with a few scratch-marks, torn clothing and bites on the girl's breasts. Naturally we need to wait for the forensic results, but from where I sit, the outlook is bleak. The police have yet to trace the boys, by the way. They called 999, gave a few details which did not include their names and left the receiver hanging in the call box.'

'Did you scratch your name on your cell wall in Winson Green?' Ralph asked, in bored mode waiting for his coffee. English ignored him.

There was a knock at the door and the familiar sound of china cups rattling. English's secretary set the tray of drinks down on a spare acre of her boss's desk and left us to it. A plate of malted milk biscuits had thoughtfully been provided. The coffee itself was contained in one of those cafetière jobs and I was relieved to see English do the honours and force down the plunger. Ralph would have sprayed the room.

'How exactly can I help you, Mr Mayo?' English said, handing cups of coffee to me and Ralph.

'Well, I'd like a copy of the prosecution file for starters,' I said, and watched Ralph lose the biscuit he was dunking in his drink. Two heavily nicotine-stained fingers retrieved the mushy remains and promptly dropped them into his lap.

'You're a messy eater, Mr Grice,' English laughed, and I swear he was holding his coffee cup with his pinky raised.

'He visits his dentist twice a year,' I said, 'to have the plaque scraped off his chin.'

English smiled. 'Leave your fax number with my secretary and I'll send a copy file through to you.'

'Do I look like I own a fax?' I said, and English got on his intercom and arranged for his secretary to photocopy the Johnson papers.

'Anything else before you go?' English was clearly tiring of our company. The feeling was mutual.

'One more thing. When you next visit Paul Johnson at Winson Green, I wanna be with you. I want to talk to him.' I noticed out of the corner of my eye Ralph brushing the soggy biscuit remains onto English's thick-pile carpet. Nice gesture, Ralph.

'Very well, Mr Mayo. Meet me outside the main prison entrance at nine-thirty tomorrow morning. If you're late I shan't wait.'

'I'll be there,' I said, standing up.

'And leave your business card with my secretary on the way out, in case I need to contact you. You do have a business card, don't you?' English was taking the piss in his own smug little way.

'Sure. And you do know how to get to Winson Green, don't you, Mr English? Oh, of course you do. You used to live there before you got a move to cushy old Sudbury. See you in the morning, then.' Ralph and I headed for the door.

In the waiting room, the secretary handed me a copy of the prosecution file.

'Remember what they say in American football, duck. It ain't over till the secretary sings.' Ralph had pressed his face right up against hers when he said that. She recoiled, naturally. Ralph's breath plays no small part in the depletion of the ozone layer.

As we walked downstairs, Ralph nudged me. 'Look what I got, Jack,' he simpered, and held up a maroon leather

Filofax. It didn't take a genius to work out who it belonged to.

'Ralph, for Christ's sake. There are certain standards to be maintained, even in this profession. We'll study it later.'

We adjourned to a local public house for a couple of pints of Bass and a bag of dry roasted peanuts. It's our idea of a power lunch. Ralph began flicking through English's Filofax. There were dozens of references to the Raphael brothers, as we'd anticipated, but nothing of any obvious use to us at that stage.

It was mid-afternoon when we got back to our office. Ralph had been more talkative on this trip, and he managed to reduce the journey time by just using the speed restrictions as a rough guide. We had trouble parking illegally outside our office, though, owing to the number of *Black & Blue* cabs dumped there.

The recession appeared to be biting harder than I thought, for even Claude's cardboard box had gone, probably repossessed. He still lay in a pool of his own, or someone else's pee, swigging from a bottle of cheap Cypriot sherry. I had a conversation with Claude once, when he was actually sober . . . ish, and he told me that as a baby, his mum had abandoned him on a stranger's doorstep. He'd made little progress since.

We got upstairs to find a note pinned to the office door: *Jack: I'm in the café along the street. Join me, Tess.* Ralph followed me like a friggin' shadow as I strolled along to the Capri. At that time of day, the place is almost respectable –if you ignore the catering aspect. The food is poor. One story had the owner, Cheesy Vic, sending a food parcel out to the starving in some African wasteland, only to get it back by return of post with a note attached saying, *We're hungry . . . but not THAT hungry.'*

During the day, the café provides cheap eats for local

workers, including Ralph. At night, its character changes. Vic has a late-night refreshment house licence and serves coffee to the fly-by-nights of society until around five o'clock in the morning. Walk in then and you'll find the café bursting at the seams with rent boys, prostitutes, pimps, transvestites, gays, mispers – missing persons, usually juveniles – thieves, burglars, lunatics let loose from their asylums by a Government keen to take advantage of care in the community, and anybody else from your worst nightmares.

Whatever the clientèle, Cheesy Vic is the perfect host. Looking older than his forty-four years, he brushes his few remaining greasy red hairs across his bald pate in a pathetic effort to look young. His front upper teeth are missing, and those remaining have taken on the colour of a neglected Victorian urinal. His pale, gaunt features give him the air of the walking dead. Vic has a penchant for teenage boys, usually rent boys, and other young men he picks up whilst importuning in the city's public lavatories. It is said, by Ralph as a matter of fact, that Vic's posterior now resembles Fingal's Cave. Anyway, Vic and I have an understanding: he's scrupulously hygienic when handling anything I might wish to consume and, in return, I won't let Ralph hurt him.

Tess was sitting at one of the dozen or so tables, each one a tribute to Formica and ingrained dirt. She was the only customer. Vic looked about as busy as the Albanian Tourist Office. Tess was staring at her empty coffee cup, her hair hanging down like a veil.

When Ralph and I sat opposite her, she looked up and smiled. 'Hi, Jack. Hi, Ralph. Did you see Mr English?' I couldn't help but notice she was wearing a black vest top which showed off her deep, milky-white cleavage. The strap had fallen down from her left shoulder, and my sweat glands began working overtime. Ralph's mouth had dropped open as he leered at Tess Johnson's ample breasts, and he was dribbling.

'We did indeed.' I looked up at the sorry figure of Cheesy and shouted, 'Three cups of your vile coffee, Vic, over here.'

'And?' she said, brushing the hair from her eyes. As she did so the flimsy, satin-type material pulled taut over her breasts and the shape of her nipples pushed through. I felt myself beginning to dribble, too.

'And I'm going to see Paul tomorrow morning at Winson Green.'

'What do you think, now you've spoken to Mr English?' Her eyes still looked puffy, but at the same time, strangely sexy.

'Things don't look good. There may even be a rape aspect to the case, now.'

'Oh, my God.' Tess brought her hands up to her face.

'Don't be alarmed. If Paul is innocent then it will be somebody else's semen at the lab. I don't think a jury would buy a theory of Michelle Rosa being unlucky enough to get raped and murdered in one night by two different men.'

'How long before we get the results?'

'They'll rush it through for a murder. Could still take a couple of weeks, though.'

Vic brought three mugs of the Turkish crap-house water he calls coffee and plonked them down on our table, then walked away without saying a word. I noticed he was wearing faded blue jeans. Vic didn't appear to have any buttocks. Still, that was the least of his problems.

'Jack, you know I suggested coming to work for you as your secretary: how about I do it for free? I'm working every night at the pub now and it's good money. I want to be involved. Please say yes.' She held her coffee mug in both hands.

I looked at Ralph. His eyes said, 'If you say no I'll kill you' so I said yes.

Tess grinned. 'Thanks, Jack. I can't just sit back and do nothing. I want to feel I'm actually doing something to help, like Jill Morrell did for John McCarthy.'

'Start tomorrow. Come and go as you please,' I said.

Tess stood up. Her other vest strap had fallen now and she made no attempt to pull them up. Today she wore tight blue jeans and canvas deck shoes which took away the height advantage of the court shoes. She did have buttocks, I noticed, as she walked out of the café.

Cheesy Vic came back to our table as Ralph and I watched Tess leaving. A cigarette which held over an inch of ash hung from the corner of his mouth. He was drying a mug with a grubby tea towel.

'She take it in the head, Jack?' he said, without moving his cigarette. I didn't dignify his question with an answer. Instead I threw some spare drachmas onto the table as payment.

'Anyone tell you that you make a great cup of coffee, Vic?' Ralph asked.

'No.'

'I'm not fuckin' surprised,' Ralph added, before getting up.

Ralph and I returned to our office. He was like a dog on heat, describing Tess Johnson's body in glowing terms. We'd only been back a couple of minutes when Diane from the sauna came in. She was in her mid-thirties and quite attractive, though, like many Greek-Cypriot women, she was beginning to accumulate the extra *avoirdupois*. Her large bosom seemed out of proportion to her height, and the bikini line on her upper lip needed some attention. On the plus side, she had flawless olive skin and shiny black hair.

'Jack, darling, have you got change for a twenty?' she said.

'Pounds or pence?' I replied.

'Pounds, of course. You don't get much for twenty pence in my place, boys.'

Diane sat on the edge of Ralph's desk while I took out my

wallet and hunted for change. She spotted the £50 notes Tess had given me. 'I thought you were supposed to be broke, Jack?'

'Who, me? I've got enough money to keep me in luxury for the rest of my life, provided I die next Tuesday,' I told her. She laughed. 'Well then, isn't it time you spent a little of it?' She leaned forward in her tasteless, low-cut leopard-skin top and put her hand in the environs of my crotch. 'See anything you like?' She ran her tongue around her lips.

That was something I could never fathom out. How come prostitutes always dress like shit? You ever driven by Balsall Heath and seen the girls hanging around the street corners, all togged up in their red Lycra mini-skirts over black fishnet tights in white stiletto-heeled shoes? It's like they all take Irma La Douce as their rôle model. Diane appeared to have taken Tarzan as hers.

'Diane, I'm a married man. Try Ralph. He's as flush as me.'

Diane turned to Ralph, who had poured himself a large glass of Scotch. 'So, Ralph. Do you feel neighbourly today?' she asked, unzipping her animal-print mini-skirt and stepping out of it. Her white panties had slipped over her curvy buttocks and lodged in the crack of her bum.

Ralph got up, knocked back his drink and led Diane out to his bedsit. He came back, moments later, in his baggy underpants, to fetch the whisky bottle. I heard Diane call him.

'I'm coming, you silly cow. Assume the fucking position.' Ralph's a real sweetie when he tries.

I took out the prosecution file and began to read the witness statements. The staff at the gym didn't do Paul any favours, that's for sure. I'd been reading for five minutes or so when the door opened. I thought it was Ralph, coming back for more whisky or a box of condoms in order to practise safe sex, but it wasn't. Two guys stood just inside the door. The one to my left was enormous, even bigger than Ralph. He was around six feet six inches tall and almost as wide. He looked the sort of guy who'd shake a tree if he got hungry. His greasy, scruffy hair exactly matched his greasy, scruffy beard. He wore a vast, once-white T-shirt and shapeless grey trousers. A hundred years ago he'd have found gainful employment with P. T. Barnum.

His pal, to my right, was quite short, maybe five feet six inches, slim with greying hair combed forward into a fringe. He had the face of a man suffering from a real bad case of Portnoy's Complaint. He wore a black studded leather jacket over blue denims with a three-inch turn up. They looked like angels – Hell's Angels. It's a sad indictment of my business, but they also looked like customers. Either that, or some of Ralph's drinking buddies.

The big guy held a Jif lemon in his right paw, although I knew it wasn't Pancake Day. The short, demonstrably ugly cohort carried a green plastic petrol can. Nice to see they were environmentally friendly.

'You Jack Mayo?' the short guy asked.

'Yes. How can I help you?' I replied.

The big oaf squeezed the lemon and stinging liquid hit me in the left eye. It felt as though acid was being used as an Optrex-substitute. I instinctively brought my hands to my face, and something hard hit me in the solar plexus. I guessed it was either the big man's fist or a low-flying aircraft. It took all the wind out of me and I struggled to breathe. Then I could smell petrol, and I felt it splash over me until I'd been drenched in unleaded. I opened my good eye and saw the little man strike a match. I waited for my life to flash before my eyes. It didn't. The little chap came too damn close for comfort with his lighted match, but then he blew it out and grinned. He had those teeth that hang down from the upper gums like decayed pear drops.

'Next time, Jack. Next time,' he said caressingly.

28

The monster then kicked me in the groin, causing my scrotum to bounce off the roof of my mouth.

'Next time, Jack, and November the Fifth comes early for you.' The smaller guy nodded to the monster and he sideswiped my face with his cupped right hand and I hit the ground like a demolished chimneystack.

I was out cold for a couple of minutes, then got up and staggered across to Ralph's bedsit. When I walked in, through my good eye I could see Ralph and Diane exercising their basic animal urges, doggy fashion. Ralph was naked but for those odd socks. Diane was nude, too, her pendulous breasts hanging down slightly further than her pendulous belly. She was the first to see me, turning her head towards me.

'Jack! You decided to join us,' she said, presumably confusing the strong smell of petrol with Ralph's repulsive body odour.

'No. I just had the excrement kicked out of me. Two goons jumped me in the office.'

Ralph turned around, from the neck, but continued rutting. He didn't mind an audience. Every time there was a police function involving a stripper, Ralph would be the one to have sex with the girl on the floor at the end of the show. He boasted how his semen could burn a hole in any carpet.

'Be with you in a minute, Jack, I'm on the vinegar strokes.' Ralph turned away and carried on with the job in hand.

I sat down in an easy chair and waited for the grunts and groans to turn into gasps and screams. When it was over Ralph got up and cracked open a post-coital can of beer. His erect penis began to lower itself like Tower Bridge. Diane got off the bed and came across to me.

'What did they do to you, Jack?' she asked, still starkers. She wasn't the sort of woman to cover her embarrassment. I found myself staring at the huge black triangle of hair between her legs and the erect, purple nipples which could take your eye out if you weren't careful.

'There were two men – one enormous beast and a short chap with bad teeth. They asked for me then squirted something in my eye. Then the big one knocked the stuffing out of me while his pal poured petrol over me. He threatened to set it alight . . . next time.'

'Who were they, Jack, do you know them?' asked Ralph, getting dressed.

'No idea, mate. I did notice one thing, though.'

'What's that?' he asked.

'English's Filofax isn't on your desk any more.'

'You reckon he sent them?'

'Pound to a pinch of shit, Ralph.'

'Maybe we ought to pay him a visit.'

'Not until after I've seen Paul Johnson in the Green.'

I felt pretty rough. Diane bathed my eye in water and tenderly massaged my face. I declined her offer to tenderly massage my balls for a tenner and left for home.

CHAPTER 3

During my career with West Midlands Police, I only got assaulted on one occasion. I managed to break the bone in my right hand after trying to rearrange the facial features of a drunken Irishman determined to throw me through the plate-glass windows of Rackham's department store. He later lodged a complaint of assault and I was formally notified on Form WG 666. Somebody in the Admin. Department probably got his rocks off sticking the Sign of the Beast on that particular form. Ralph, I may say, picked up enough of these in his career to have papered the walls of a four-bedroomed house.

Fighting was part of the job, though I was never very good at it. Ralph, on the other hand, was a master practitioner. Every Friday and Saturday night the Brummies would come into town to play. Armed with their giro cash, they'd desert their council homes and swamp the city centre in search of a good time. That 'good time' usually entailed sinking a dozen pints of beer, copping a feel of some peroxide-blonde slut and puking up after downing a greasy kebab. After a really good time, you could smash a shop window and get yourself arrested. Such is the sophisticated night life of the second city.

A Brum is easily spotted. He's low IQ, high-sperm-count material, usually clad in a cap-sleeve Ouzo-power T-shirt from which his weedy arms hang like pipe cleaners, and with espadrilles on his feet. This, in a January snowstorm.

At closing time, Brums spill out onto the streets and start fighting. The traditional Brummie greeting of a beer glass in the face is over-employed to keep casualty staff on their toes at the Accident Hospital. Fights break out in chip-shops, on the top decks of night service buses, in the waiting rooms of taxi firms, at the police station, in the hospitals and, of course, that old favourite . . . the curry houses. Some bobby always has to wade in and sort it out. Ralph revelled in all of this, of course. Somebody at Complaints once asked him why he'd ever joined the police and Ralph, mindful of the fact that he was being investigated for yet another assault, allegedly replied, 'Because I like to work with my hands.'

I'd had a restless night. Alison, my wife, was upset to see I'd been assaulted. She thought all that had finished when I left the police. We've been married eight years and we're already in separate beds. Rudolf Hess had a more active sex life whilst in Spandau than I have now. I lay back and thought of the two goons who'd whacked me, of Ralph and his curious sexual technique and mostly, of Tess and her heaving white bosom. At six o'clock I got out of bed and showered. By seven-thirty I was back at the office. There was a smell of man-fat about the place and I wondered if Ralph had invited Diane to straddle one or other of the desks whilst they practised the Apollo Eleven docking manoeuvre. The pair of white knickers hanging from the coat-stand were the big giveaway.

I drove through the rush-hour traffic to Winson Green Prison, and parked my '88 VW Golf in Foundry Road, underneath one of those clever-dick ads for Silk Cut ciggies. I walked the couple of hundred yards to the main prison entrance. It was already hot enough to drape my jacket over my shoulders. There was a visitor centre opposite the prison, like you'd find at a safari park or a National Trust stately home. The prison itself, hidden behind twenty-feet-high brick walls, was built in 1849. In the 1980s the Home Office broke into a fiver to refurbish the place. The entrance was now a high-tech affair in dark blue, contrasting with the red brick and corrugated sheeting elsewhere. The entrance resembled a giant condiment set, its two domed hexagonal pods a scaled-down version of Wembley's twin towers. Ralph would probably describe the same structure as two phallic symbols. The *Dieu et mon droit* coat of arms hung above the entrance door, as did a CCTV camera. I was twenty minutes early, so I waited across the road.

I read once that Winson Green nick had had a bad reputation even back in the 1850s, when it was known as the Birmingham Borough Gaol. The warders, then, used to like to use strait-jackets, 'the crank', and deprivation of food in order to keep control. Happy days.

As a detective, I'd visited Winson Green many times, to get 'write-offs'. We'd visit convicted villains and they'd tell us about other crimes they'd committed whilst free and for which they had never been charged. In return for forty fags and a Mars Bar you could write off a hundred crimes a day. Naturally, this paid dividends when the crime clearance rates were published. The Home Office approved. One sub-division ended up with a clearance rate in excess of 100 per cent over one quarter of the year. Then the wheel came off and the Home Office suddenly about-faced and decided it didn't approve after all.

Eddie English arrived, looking good and cool in a grey flannel double-breasted suit and carrying a hard shell briefcase. A rolled-up copy of a pink newspaper was tucked under his arm.

'What happened to you?' he said, in lieu of 'Good morning.'

'Some blokes have got "come to bed eyes". I've got "step outside eyes". I must have upset somebody.'

33

'Does it hurt?'

'Not really. I've narrowed it down to five hundred suspects. It's the nature of the job. Shall we go inside? You still got your keys?'

'It was a long time ago, Jack,' he said.

'Sorry, Eddie. Just that I've never worked with a solicitor who had a CRO number before. You aren't carrying anything I ought to know about, are you? A flick-knife, or set of knuckle-dusters, the jawbone of an ass . . . that sort of thing?'

Eddie ignored me and led us inside. We were frisked by the prison officers in their monochrome uniforms before passing through submarine locks and airport-style X-ray machines. Confident, finally, that we weren't from Crime Inc. – well, at least I wasn't, I couldn't speak for English – the guard took us into a glass-walled interview room. He didn't appreciate my crack about us bringing in a file but not having time to bake the cake; even when I explained I meant the prosecution file.

The interview room, one of several on either side of this corridor, was sparsely furnished. If there had been a condom machine on the wall it would have reminded me of Ralph's bedsit. There was a table and three chairs. I sat down. English took off his jacket and draped it over the back of his chair. Within a few moments, a guard had led Paul Johnson into the room.

He was a good-looking chap in his middle to late twenties, with a muscular torso and a trendy shaven haircut. He'd be very popular in here if he got sent down. The boys would be fighting to give him a seminal enema.

'Have a seat, Paul. This is Jack Mayo. I think you know your wife has hired him to track down Michelle's killer.' English pointed to me like I was hidden in a crowd.

I shook Johnson's hand and we all sat down. Johnson, on remand, had the privilege of dressing in his own clothes. He wore a grey and black shell suit.

34

'For Mr Mayo's benefit, Paul, let's hear your version of events from the very beginning.' English took out a foolscap writing pad and a chubby tortoiseshell fountain pen and began taking notes. I just listened.

'Okay. I worked as an instructor at the Amazon Gym in Lichfield, which is owned by a guy called Barry Raphael. The place is deliberately decked out in pink and pastel shades to attract women rather than men, so we get a lot of female bodybuilders who sometimes feel rather intimidated in the normal male-dominated gyms. There's a couple of other guys working there, plus several women. Two or three months ago, a new girl started work with us as an aerobics teacher. That was Michelle Rosa.'

Johnson was nervous. I'm not sure what was shaking the most, his hands or his voice.

'Anyway, sometimes I'd be working out or taking a class and I'd look up and Michelle would be staring at me. I took no notice at first. Then, about three weeks ago, after the last class had finished and everyone else had gone, I went for a shower. Next thing I knew, Michelle had joined me in the shower. She had nothing on and began kissing me and rubbing my dick. I got out of the shower and told her it just wasn't on, that I was married and she should look elsewhere for her kicks. From then on there was no problem. It was like the incident had never happened.'

Paul was very dark, with almost black hair. His eyebrows met and I remembered my mum telling me something about men whose eyebrows met. He carried on.

'Last Tuesday evening, I didn't have the car as Tess had used it to go to Birmingham for a hen party. I intended to jog home to Burntwood, but Michelle heard about this and said it was too dangerous in the dark, especially as there are no footpaths for much of the way. She offered me a lift and I accepted. At about eleven p.m. she dropped me off outside my house and I never saw her again. Then, last Thursday

35

morning the police broke down my door and arrested me for murder. That's all there is, Mr Mayo.'

'Any questions, Jack?' English asked.

'Yeah, plenty. Did you find Michelle attractive, Paul?'

'I'm a married man, Mr Mayo,' Johnson said.

'What sort of fucking answer is that? In six months you're gonna be alone in a witness box at Stafford Crown Court while some overpaid prosecution counsel begins feeding you to the twelve good men and true of the jury. You give that sort of noncommittal answer and the next thing you know is you've got a lifetime job pruning the Governor's roses.' I don't like to be pissed about.

'Sorry. Yes, of course I fancied her. She was very attractive. All the girls at the gym are, except maybe a few of the heavier female bodybuilders.'

'So you're telling me that a girl you fancy climbs into your shower bollock-naked and all you do is climb out?' Ralph would deem Johnson a poofter on the basis of that evidence alone.

'I know it's hard to believe, but that's how it was. You've met Tess, Mr Mayo. I've no need to go with other women.'

It was a valid point.

'Okay, so last Tuesday she offered you a lift home, which you gratefully accepted. She dropped you off and that was it?' I asked.

'Yes.'

'No goodnight kiss or anything?'

'No. Maybe a peck on the cheek, that's all.'

'And then she drove off?'

'Yes. I went indoors, had a protein drink and went to bed.'

'Are you being totally honest with me, Paul?'

'What do you mean, Mr Mayo?'

'When Michelle's body was found she had recently had sex. Now if what you say is true, you've got nothing to worry about because, never having had sex with Michelle, it couldn't possibly be your semen in her vagina, your pubic hairs mixed with hers, your skin under her fingernails. Shall I continue?'

He began to look flustered and moved around on his seat like it was a hotplate.

'All right, I did have sex with Michelle.'

'When?'

'Several times. In the shower to start with, then every night after the gym closed, usually on a workout mat or across a bench. Last Tuesday, it was back at my place, as Tess was away. We had sex three or four times then she left at about two a.m. I didn't kill her, Mr Mayo.'

'What you got form for, kid?' I asked.

'How do you know I've got form?'

'Because your fingerprints must be on record for the police to have been able to match them up with those on the knife.'

'Four years ago, when I was broke, I bought a stolen chequebook and card off a bloke in a pub. I got nicked the first time I tried to use it. That was the one and only time.'

'The way I see it, Paul, there are two possibilities. One, you're as guilty as sin and a proficient liar. Two, you're as innocent as you say you are and you're the subject of the best stitching job since the Bayeux Tapestry.' I looked him in the eye.

'Which do you think, Mr Mayo?' he asked.

'I'll let you know,' I said.

'Can I ask you both a favour?' he said.

'Go on.'

'Don't tell Tess about my fling with Michelle. Let me do it.'

'It's your business, mate,' I shrugged, adding, 'If you didn't murder Michelle, then who wanted her dead – and why? Can you assist us with that?'

'No. It just doesn't add up at all.'

'What can you tell me about Michelle?' I asked.

'Very little. Our relationship was pure sex, no strings attached.'

'Well, where did she live, did she have a boyfriend, other family, was she friendly with anybody else at the gym, what was her background? Need I go on?' I said.

'I know this sounds odd, Mr Mayo, but I really don't know the answers to any of those questions. You could try asking Beverley.'

'Who's she?'

'Beverley Calvert. She's the female body-building instructor at the gym. She's also Barry Raphael's personal fitness trainer.'

'Where does she live?'

'With Barry and his wife out at Lower Longdon, just off the A51 Lichfield to Rugeley Road.'

'Is she Raphael's bit on the side?' I asked.

'He's married.'

'Didn't stop you,' I said.

'No. You're probably right. She's a real stunner.'

'As a matter of fact,' I said, 'the name Beverley Calvert rings a bell. There's a copy statement made by her in the prosecution file. I think I'm correct in saying that, according to her, you continually tried it on with her and Michelle and they both gave you the brush-off. She further stated that you were besotted with Michelle and couldn't keep your hands off her. According to Beverley, Michelle intended to leave the gym because of you.'

'It's not true. If anything, it was the other way round.'

'She's not the only one at the gym to say all of this. Were you on good terms with your colleagues?' I asked.

'Absolutely. We were a real close bunch. What's going to happen to me, Mr Mayo?'

'Well, you're in it up to your traps, Paul. When the police

get the forensic results they'll think Christmas arrived early. I assume you denied having sex with Michelle when interviewed?'

Johnson nodded.

'There's a lot of evidence against you, Paul. The fingerprints on the murder weapon, for instance. How do you account for that?'

'It was my knife. I kept it at the gym to do various jobs.'

'Her panties in your locker?'

'I don't know. I'm not that stupid.'

'Your T-shirt in her car?'

'That's possible. We began tearing each other's clothes off before the car even came to a halt.' He leaned forward with his head in his hands.

'There's just one thing the police don't have,' I said, by way of encouragement.

'What's that?' Johnson asked.

'A motive. Only psychopaths kill without one and you're not a psychopath – are you?'

'No.'

'If you're guilty, Paul, life imprisonment is nothing. If you're innocent, it's a hell of a fucking time.' I stood up and put my jacket on.

'Can you get me out of here, Mr English?'

'I'll apply for bail when you're next up on Friday morning.'

'What are my chances?'

'Zero.' English didn't beat about the bush. 'You're here until the trial, I'm afraid – unless Mr Mayo turns up something to point the finger elsewhere.'

'I'm counting on you, Mr Mayo.'

English stood up and picked up his jacket. A guard came and led Johnson away. English and I walked off, hardly speaking to each other. It turned out he had parked his car next to mine.

Finally, I had to know.

'Well, Eddie – do you think your client is guilty?'

'Yes, I do. The weight of evidence, even without a motive, is crippling. When we add the forensic and anything else they might find, Paul can consider himself a goner.'

'I think the kid's innocent, or the dumbest fucker who ever walked this earth. Nobody ever left this many clues, even for Miss Marple.'

We got back to the cars. Some passing thief had smashed in the driver's window of English's midnight-blue seven series BMW.

'Anything taken, Ed?' I asked, not really caring.

'My portable telephone. CD player. CDs. My wax cotton jacket. They've even taken the tax disc.'

'Tough break,' I said, climbing into my Golf and driving off.

CHAPTER 4

It was lunchtime when I got back to my office. I knew it was lunchtime because Ralph was still eating breakfast at his desk. He was devouring a thick, greasy bacon buttie and slurping down a mug of coffee. I was rather taken aback to see that he had shaved, probably even showered, and changed into his summer wardrobe, which consists of his Romanian suit trousers and a beige sports jacket which doesn't go even close to fitting him. It looks like he got it off the peg. Norman Wisdom's peg.

Tess was stood near the tea-makings, trying to dislodge a spoon which had stuck fast to the tray. She was wearing a coral-coloured sundress which came to a halt several inches above her knees. It was made of that stretchy material which hugs every curve of the body like clingfilm. The two straps crossed at the back. She wasn't wearing a bra beneath it and there was no visible pantie line. Her shoes were coral to match the dress. Tess smiled at me and asked if I wanted a coffee. I diverted my eyes from her thighs and nodded.

'Did you speak to Paul, Jack?' she asked.

'I did.'

'And?'

'We went through the whole business, from the start.'

'Now you've listened to his version of events, do you think he's guilty?' She handed me a mug of too-milky coffee.

'No, I don't. English does, however, which is somewhat disconcerting. My advice, Tess, is that you should change Paul's defence brief. If I was going to Crown Court on a murder rap I'd want counsel to have been advised by somebody who believes in me.'

'Paul doesn't qualify for legal aid so it would mean using every penny of our savings. Our Greek dream would go up in smoke.'

'Tess, the prosecution evidence is good. Suffice it to say it's getting better by the minute. Paul needs a solicitor who's on his side. If you stick with English, your husband will go down the steps for sure. Where does that leave Greece?'

She brushed her hair out of her eye, while Ralph belched. Unusually for him, he said, 'Pardon me.'

'You're right, Jack. Do you know anybody better than English who we could hire?'

'What about Noddy Jacobs?' asked Ralph.

'Serious answers, on a postcard only, Ralph,' I replied.

'I'm being serious. Okay, he's past his best but he's the toughest old git who ever cross-examined me in the box. He's as straight as it's possible to be in the legal profession, and he might come to a financial arrangement to suit you, Tess.'

'Jacobs is a drunk,' I said.

'Nothing wrong with liking a tot or two. He's a damn good lawyer, Jack.' Ralph threw the bread-crusts into a waste bin near the door. His poor aim left one in the bin, one on the floor and one hanging from a bookshelf. He wiped his hands on a piece of pink blotting paper.

Tess sat on the edge of Ralph's desk, with her back to him. One leg stretched to the floor to support her weight while the other dangled. Her dress rode high up her thighs. I felt a stirring in my groin.

'Well, Jack. Can we go and see him?' she asked, playfully balancing her shoe on her toes.

'It's your money,' I said, 'but that can wait until tomorrow. In the meantime I want to visit Michelle's home and then see this girl called Beverley at Paul's gym. Ralph, I've got a job for you, too.'

'What might that be, Jack?' Ralph asked.

'Remember Terry Smith, the old beat bobby? Retired about six or seven years ago. He knew everybody up the town. Give him a bell, take him for a drink or ten and pump him for as much info as you can get on the Raphael brothers. Take a notepad and pen, your memory ain't what it was. Oh, and keep a note of your spending for expenses.'

'It's dirty work, Jack, but somebody's got to do it. Where does Terry live?'

'Out in the sticks – Bridgnorth way, I think. I believe he runs a little country pub.'

'Bliss,' said Ralph. 'I'll find him.'

'Your face is bruised. What happened to you?' Tess touched my face gently.

'I had visitors last night. Well, late afternoon, actually. Two guys came in asking for directions and took offence when I asked for a fee. It doesn't hurt much any more. Right – time to get cracking!'

'Can I come with you, Jack? I want to be involved.'

How could I refuse? She looked better than Ralph, and the smell of her perfume, *Amarige* by Givenchy – I saw the box in her handbag – was a nice change from Ralph's gruesome odour.

'Yeah. Okay. Ready to go?'

She bent over, straight-legged, and picked up her handbag. The thin material of her dress stretched over the fleshy mounds of her buttocks. Ralph looked at me. I looked at him. We shared the same thought bubble.

'Shame about English's car,' Ralph said suddenly.

'What do you mean?' I asked.

'Let's just say, "wait till he opens the glove compartment".'

43

'Why?' I asked, immediately wishing I hadn't.

'It's full of dog shit,' grinned Ralph. 'Stinks to hell in this weather.'

Ralph was still a schoolboy in a grown man's body. This was his little victory against 'that bastard English' as my partner liked to call him.

Declining Tess's kind offer to cram my six feet two inches into her Mini, we got into the Golf, which was hot enough inside to bake bread. I drove off along Stratford Road towards City while Tess switched on the radio and wound down her window. If her dress had ridden much higher you'd have sworn it was a scarf. I kept one eye on the road and one eye on her shapely legs as we picked our way through the traffic. A million people live in Birmingham, of whom approximately nine hundred thousand are minicab drivers.

'Where are we going first?' Tess asked, checking her make-up in the vanity mirror behind the sun visor.

'Newtown. According to the papers English gave me, Michelle lived here with her boyfriend. At any rate, this is the last address we have for her. She's a bit of a mystery girl.'

Some minutes later I parked the car at the foot of twenty-storey Lech Walesa House in the unfortunately-named Coconut Grove. Any resemblance to Florida was purely coincidental. Leaving the Golf between a Mark Three Cortina which was propped up on house-bricks rather than wheels, and the burned-out shell of a Renault Five, we went inside the tower block which the council had swathed in canvas sheets and scaffolding as part of a drive to prevent concrete cladding falling on the residents.

There was no concierge at this block and it was as neglected and about as desirable a domicile as Claude's old box. We took the lift, which the last occupant had forgotten to flush, up to the fifteenth floor. Flat 61 had an unpainted replacement door, as had most of the flats, courtesy of countless previous burglaries. In contrast to the heat outside, the corridor was dark and cool, almost cold. I knocked on the door which had number 61 scrawled on it in white chalk, next to the statement 'Darren is a twat', recorded in black marker pen.

There was no reply. I looked through the letterbox, but no sign of life stirred inside. It was probably a giro-drop. I knocked again. A male voice shouted from inside: 'Who is it?'

'It's the police,' I said. It wasn't so much a lie, more a piece of information that was out of date.

We waited as the male undid half a dozen locks, bolts and chains. When the door opened, a scrawny-looking youth stood there, holding a can of Evo-Stik. His eyes were the eyes of a determined glue-sniffer. His teeth were the colour of the Sheffield Wednesday away strip and his wiry frame was covered in tattoos, including, I noticed, the usual *ACAB – all coppers are bastards –* on the knuckles of the hand gripping the glue. He wasn't the sort of guy you'd want to dip into the fondue with.

'What the fuck do you want now?' he asked sympathetically.

'I'm Detective Sergeant Mayo from Cheapside Police. This is WDC Johnson. We want to ask some questions about Michelle Rosa. Can we come in?'

'How long's this gonna take?' he asked.

'The longer we stand out here, the longer it's going to take,' I said, noticing the mucus escaping from both his nostrils. He wore a white vest top and denim shorts, together with flip-flops. He'd have looked the picture of health in Belsen.

He beckoned us inside. The flat stank like a colostomy bag with a slow puncture. There was nothing inside you could describe as furniture. He led us to a room which had a double mattress on the floor and matching Kentucky Fried Chicken boxes as bedside tables. It was the hovel of an under-achiever. Luckily, he didn't have enough social skill to offer us refreshments. I opened a window.

'So this is where Michelle lived, is it?' I asked.

'She stayed here for one night, about a month ago, that's all.'

'Were you her boyfriend, then?' Tess asked.

The scumbag laughed and sniffed at the same time. 'Not bloody likely. I'm her step-brother.'

'What's your name?' I asked.

'I've been asked all this already.'

'Now I'm asking again.'

'Darren Tonks.'

Darren the twat.

'How are you related, then? Talk me through it,' I said.

'Michelle's mum is my mum, but we've got different dads.'

'Is your mum still alive?' Tess asked.

'Far as I know. She still hawks her mutton down Balsall Heath.'

'A prostitute?'

'You're fast. When Michelle's dad left our mum, she was forced to go on the game. I'm the result of one of the many times Mum got fuckin' raped by a punter. My dad could be any one of about two thousand blokes. Done well for myself, ain't I?'

'Did you keep in touch with Michelle over the years?' I asked.

'Nah. She moved to the Smoke. Last month was the first time I'd seen her in years. Christ knows how she found me. Now she's dead. They've got the cunt who killed her, probably get a soddin' community service order.'

'What did Michelle talk about when she stayed the night? Apart from complimenting you on the décor?' I asked.

46

'She went on about getting revenge on somebody. I can't really remember 'cos I'd been hitting the glue pretty bad when she arrived. Look, if you don't mind, I have to go out.'

'I'm not a cop, Darren. I'm a private detective. I've been hired to find out who really killed your step-sister. I need your help. Here's my card.' I handed him a cheap and nasty business card from a machine in the Bull Ring.

'Like I said, I got to go out. But if I think of anything else, I'll let you know,' he looked at the card, 'Mr Mayo.'

Tess and I left the place Darren called home, contrary to the Trades Descriptions Act, and headed out to the car.

I opened the door for her and watched her dress ride up again as she climbed inside. We headed off to Lichfield, going through Kingstanding and Streetly before picking up the A5127 at Blake Street. Tess dozed off in the heat. The sun reflected off the rear windscreens of the cars in front. I loosened my tie and undid my top shirt button. The spires of Lichfield Cathedral loomed up ahead through the shimmering heat haze.

The Amazon Gym was set in a side road, just off Beacon Street. It looked like it had been converted from an old car showroom, being a two-storey building with a flat roof and large plate-glass windows. In Birmingham it could have won an architectural award. But so, too, could a Portakabin.

The building was coloured a pastel shade of pink, and a neon light lit up the words *Amazon Gym*. Two huge palm trees made of plastic or fibreglass skirted the double entrance doors and a two-dimensional Amazon lady with muscles like Arnold and a costume like Cher acted as a twelve-feet-high logo on the fascia. Lichfield City Planning Committee must have missed this one. It was more Las Vegas than English country town. This is Lichfield. *It is genteel.* Even Ronald McDonald has to wear a wax cotton jacket over his red and yellow clown suit. Talking of clown suits, I wondered how Ralph was getting on.

I smiled when I thought of the time he'd blagged a rookie cop into giving the kiss of life to a six-week-old corpse. Ralph was the man who conducted the initiation ceremonies on the unit. Male probationers had to stand on a bar stool with their trousers and pants round their ankles and their genitals shoved into a pint of beer. That was known as 'displacement'. Females were put over Ralph's knees, their panties removed and the station rubber stamp daubed all over their backsides. I told you he was a class act.

I woke Tess and waited a moment or so until she had regained her composure.

'Leave the talking to me, love. If anybody asks, we're husband and wife and you're thinking of joining the gym – okay?'

'You're the boss,' she said, smiling.

We entered the gym. There was a counter in the foyer and aluminium-framed photographs of the top bodybuilders. All women: Cory Everson, Rachel McLish, Bev Francis, Tina Plakinger, all in flexed poses. The counter obviously doubled as a sort of café, with various drinks and protein powders on sale. I knew a bit about bodybuilding, having been a regular down at the police station multi-gym before my knee went wonky. I never got to look like Schwarzenegger but then, I never had his dedication. There was a pretty girl behind the counter wearing a pink polo shirt bearing the Amazon Gym logo over her left breast, such as it was. She looked up from whatever she'd been doing. Her blonde hair was natural and cut short in a bob. As she smiled, her green eyes smiled too, which I found appealing.

'Can I help you?' she asked.

'My wife is considering joining the gym. We wondered if we could check out the facilities,' I said smoothly.

'Certainly. I'll get one of the girls to show you round.' She picked up the phone and made a brief internal call, requesting somebody called Vanessa to make her way to reception. In the meantime she practised her sales patter.

'It costs four hundred and twenty pounds to join, which is a once-only life membership payment of seventy pounds plus your yearly fee of three hundred and fifty pounds. You can pay all at once or on a monthly basis. There are no hidden costs thereafter. Everything is free – jacuzzi, sauna, weights, aerobic classes, even the sunbeds. Alternatively, you can become a life member for seventy pounds and pay three pounds per individual gym session.'

I was relieved to see the girl Vanessa walk through the swing doors. I was more than relieved, I was stunned. She was fresh from a work-out. Her too-brown skin had a cover of sweat and her skimpy black leotard looked like it had been fashioned from one of Moshe Dayan's old eye-patches. It left very little to my overworked imagination. It was so high-cut on the legs that there was just a thin strand of material separating the leg-hole from the arm-hole. Cut deep at the chest, it appeared to be held together by the wide, white-leather weightlifting belt she wore. Her thick ankle socks and cross-trainers seemed oddly out of place.

'Hi! I'm Vanessa. Let me show you round. This way, please.'

She swivelled and walked back towards the swing doors. Her leotard made no attempt to cover her brown buttocks. Her legs were hard and well-muscled, as were her arms. Veins stood out from places they had no right to stand out from. She had the V-shaped torso craved by bodybuilders and a waist you could fit in a Smartie tube. Call me a weirdo, but I found her attractive. Her ash-blonde hair looked like it had been fashioned by the Royal Engineers in a controlled explosion, but she had a doll of a face. I'd have followed her anywhere. In the event she took us into the main gym.

It was expensively equipped with dozens of Nautilus-style weight machines, pieces of metalwork that could exercise every part of your body – like lat machines, squat machines, sit-up benches, fly machines, leg presses, bench presses. There were also free weights and a selection of dumb-bells, bars, ropes, wall-bars, lots of full-length mirrors and a clientèle that would have had Ralph beating his meat in the car park.

I saw just one man, and he was clearly an instructor. He was a black man built like the Town Hall. Everywhere else I looked were women in varying states of undress, sweating, pumping iron, encouraging each other to lift that last rep or posing in front of the mirrors. I thought I'd died in my sleep and the swing doors were the Pearly Gates. My throat had dried up and the moisture seemed to have relocated in my armpits. Sweat ran down my sides, soaking my shirt.

'This is the main gym area, as you can see. There are always at least two qualified instructors on duty. We have just about every type of muscle machine currently on the market.' Vanessa launched into her rehearsed speech mode.

I concentrated on the bodies in the gym, including Vanessa's. I noticed she had designer stubble around her crotch where she'd obviously had to shave her pubic hair to make herself look decent in her costume. I must confess it fascinated me. Everywhere I looked, muscles bulged.

Vanessa took us through more swing doors into another large room where a well-attended aerobics class was in progress, exercising to an up-tempo Laura Branigan tune. I ignored the patter.

Through more swing doors, into a corridor and through a single swing door. Once inside, Vanessa said, 'These are the changing rooms,' about the same time as a naked black girl came from behind a stack of lockers, smiled and disappeared.

'The showers are through there and every member has their own full-size locker,' Vanessa recited, as a nude woman came out of the showers, drying her hair with her towel. I had a hard on which I hoped to God nobody noticed. It gave me a peculiar way of walking.

Vanessa hadn't finished yet. She led us upstairs to the sauna rooms, the jacuzzis and the sunbeds. Wherever I looked I saw young, attractive women, either partly dressed or totally naked. None of them objected to my presence. I wanted to stay. It was worth every last penny of four hundred and twenty quid.

'Is Beverley Calvert in today?' I asked, trying to get back to business.

'You know Beverley?' Vanessa enquired.

'Only by name. Somebody mentioned her when we said we were coming here today.'

'Today's her day off. You'll find she's over at the boss's house. She acts as his personal trainer too.'

'Who is the boss?' I asked, even though I knew.

'Mr Raphael. He lives at Lower Longdon in The Old Schoolhouse.' She had a mole at the top of her left thigh. A gentlemen wouldn't have noticed that.

'Did you work with Michelle Rosa?' I asked.

'Yes. She was murdered last week. Look, who are you? You're not here to join the gym, are you?'

'No. In the words of George Washington, "I cannot tell a lie". I'm a private detective. This is Mrs Johnson. Her husband Paul is alleged to have killed Michelle.'

'I think you'd better go. We've all made statements to the police and I don't want to get involved.'

'If you made a statement, you're already involved,' I said, in a matter-of-fact manner. 'This Michelle — did she really have a crush on Paul Johnson, or was it the other way round like you all said in your statements?' I added.

'If you don't go, I'll call the police,' she said.

I felt there was little to be gained by pressing her at this point. Besides, I needed some fresh air.

'We're going. Here's my card if you want to talk. Any

time. No need to dress, I prefer informality.' I handed her a card bearing a coffee ring. I suggested to Ralph once that, in deference to him, our logo should be identical to the Olympic symbol, but consisting of five coffee rings. He farted at the suggestion and I took that to be a negative reaction.

Tess and I left the premises and stood by the Golf. Tess fished a pair of sunglasses from the enormous handbag she carried everywhere and put them on.

'Do you find those bodybuilders attractive, Jack?' she asked.

'Yes, I must admit I do.'

We got into the car and drove off.

'Jack, can we go via my house? I'll fix us both a drink – I'm really thirsty.'

'Why not?' I said, taking the Walsall Road out of Lichfield, towards Burntwood. Tess lived, as I'd expected, in a semi about a hundred yards from Swan Island. It was neat with a tidy front garden and a black cast-metal house sign saying *Limenas*. She caught me looking at it.

'That's the place where Paul and I hope to start our business. It's the town on the island of Thassos. I adore the place.'

We went indoors and I followed Tess straight through the hall and out the back to the paved patio area.

'What would you like to drink? Whisky, vodka, beer?'

'Beer would be nice,' I said.

Tess disappeared indoors, and I sat down in one of those chunky white resin garden seats, facing a small fish-pond. Tess re-emerged with two ice-cold bottles of German lager and two glasses. She poured the beer and handed me one, then lay on the resin sun-lounger.

'What's next, Jack?'

She'd kicked off her shoes and I noticed her toenails were painted the same dark shade of red as her fingernails.

'I'll call on Raphael, see if this Beverley girl is there. Tomorrow morning we'll pay a visit to Noddy Jacobs, ask if he'll represent your husband.'

'Do you mind if I don't come with you to Raphael's? I'm feeling tired and I'm working at the pub tonight.'

'Of course not. As a matter of fact, that suits me better. I'm going to pose as a cop again and you look nothing like any WDC I ever saw. Not dressed like that.'

'Will you let me know the outcome?' she asked, raising her sunglasses so they rested on her head, 'before you go back to Birmingham?'

'Yeah. Sure I will.' I finished my drink and got up to go.

'Jack, will you give me a lift in tomorrow? My car's still in Brum.'

'Pick you up at eight.'

It was late afternoon when I arrived at The Old School House, Lower Longdon. I'd expected Barry Raphael's home to be given a quaint name, like *Dunthievin'* or something similar. Instead, I found the sort of period residence you dream of owning. Whoever said crime doesn't pay never met the Raphaels. Set back off the little country lane, the house was reached up a fifty-yard gravel drive. I parked in the lane.

Part of the house was timbered and probably dated back to the days when Lord Brooke managed to get himself shot in Dam Street. I guessed it was a listed building and probably worth close to three hundred grand. There were a couple of acres of land with the place. Very nice. You could imagine our local hero Dr Johnson riding out of here for a swift beverage after a tough day teaching at Edial.

I rang the doorbell and was pleasantly surprised to find that it didn't play *Colonel Bogey*. The door opened and a little oriental woman stood at the step. She looked like a cross between Cory Aquino and Oddjob from *Goldfinger*.

I held up an old West Midlands Travel bus pass and said, 'Police. Detective Jack Mayo. Is Mr Raphael in?'

'No. He out jogging.'

'What about Miss Calvert?'

'She in, out back. You can't come in.'

'You a Filipino? Can I see your work permit?' I asked.

'You go round back. Miss Calvert at the swimming pool.' She closed the door.

I followed the building line around the back, via a gravel path flanked by mature shrubs and bushes. When it turned into block paving I knew I was getting close to patio-land. I walked through a doorway in a six-feet-high wall and found myself on a paved terrace around the large rectangular swimming pool. The turquoise water looked inviting. Shading my eyes from the still-hot sun I made my way across to where Beverley lay face-down on a sun-lounger. I knew it was her since there was nobody else about, apart from an old guy tending the flowerbeds nearby.

Beverley wore a cream Panama hat, sunglasses, a gold ankle chain and nothing else. It was one of those days. She was reading a dog-eared paperback and listening to her Walkman. As I approached from the direction of her feet, she neither saw nor heard me. I studied her naked body for a few seconds before I spoke. Actually it was more like twenty minutes but I was in no hurry.

She had long black hair and a tall, sleek, lightly tanned body. It was an all-over tan as far as I could see. And I could see far. I felt like asking the old gardener if he needed an assistant. Beverley was muscular, but in a more aesthetically pleasing way than Vanessa. I coughed but got no reaction.

I moved closer, where she could see my feet. She took off the Walkman and her Wayfarers and looked up at me. She wasn't the slightest bit embarrassed. I was. I mopped my brow with my hanky.

54

Her body glistened under the film of Ambre Solaire. She took off her last remaining vestige of dignity, her Panama, and lifted herself up onto her elbows.

'And who might you be?' she asked.

She had a long face with dark brown, almond-shaped eyes and full, luscious lips. As well as her ankle chain, I saw she was wearing gold earrings, a gold horn-of-plenty on a chain around her neck, various gold bracelets and several rings. So I convinced myself she wasn't quite fully unclothed.

'I might be Kilroy, come to write on your lavatory wall. But I'm not.'

'You're not the police again, are you?' she asked.

'No. I'm a private investigator.'

'Who let you in?'

'Imelda Marcos. I told her I was a shoe salesman. I need to ask you some questions, Miss Calvert.'

'Fix me a drink, will you, Mr . . . ?'

'Mayo. Jack Mayo.'

'Have one yourself. Mine's an orange juice.'

I walked across to the little white resin trolley and poured two orange juices. When I turned round, Beverley was standing naked and rubbing the excess oil from her tummy. I had never seen such a gorgeous body. It was the body of a centre-fold, the sort of girls who don't exist in real life. I looked at her firm breasts, and the two goose-pimply claret-coloured nipples protruding, as Ralph would say, 'like organ-stops', from the flawless golden skin. My eyes lowered to her flat stomach and the delta of bushy black pubic hair. I was in a trance. This was all too much in one day.

'If you could tear your eyes from my crotch, Mr Mayo, perhaps you could hand me that top, behind you.'

I reluctantly tore my eyes from her crotch and grabbed the lime-green vest top from the handle of the trolley. I took a long, last look at her body before she slipped the baggy top on. I hoped I'd burned that vision into my memory for those long winter nights ahead. I handed her the remains of her drink from my shaking hand and sat down at another lounger.

Beverley's vest top reached nearly as far as her knees, which was a major disappointment, but the arm-holes and neck-hole were so generously cut, they barely managed to cover anything. I was getting that dry-throat feeling again.

'How well do you know Paul Johnson, Miss Calvert?' I asked.

'I've been through all this, Mr Mayo.'

'It is important. Most murders are. His wife hired me to find out who really killed Michelle Rosa.'

Beverley laughed. 'Then she's wasting her money. Paul was infatuated with Michelle like he was infatuated with anything in a skirt . . . or preferably out of a skirt. Michelle didn't want to know and it must have hurt his mighty ego.' She sipped her drink whilst sitting on the edge of the lounger. Then she readjusted the position so the lounger would support her back and stretched out, facing me.

'Was he infatuated with you?' I asked.

'Of course. And we had an affair. He's a very attractive man.'

'Was he married at the time?' I mumbled.

'Yes. And he was married when he screwed Vanessa and a dozen or so of the gym's members. He's a real stud, our Mr Johnson.' She stretched her arms behind her head. Nicely shaved armpits, I thought.

'Why did Michelle spurn his advances, then, do you think?'

'You really don't know what's been going on, do you?' she asked, with a smile. 'Michelle, Mr Mayo, is or rather was, a lesbian. She was what the guys call "drop dead gorgeous" but it didn't alter the fact that she only had eyes

56

for women. It never affected her work though. She kept her private life separate from work.'

'What are you saying, then – that the rebuff dented Paul's masculine pride and that he subsequently raped her and killed her?' I finished my drink. Orange juice is lost without vodka.

'I have no idea. Can you come up with another motive?'

'According to Paul, it was all the other way round. Michelle tried to seduce him. She turned up in his shower, by all accounts.'

'If you don't believe me, Mr Mayo, why don't you ask her girlfriend?'

'Who is she?' I asked.

'Vanessa Lewis. They lived together. It was Vanessa who got her the job at the gym.'

'Where does she live?'

'I can't tell you that. You'll have to ask her. Now, if you don't mind, I'd like to take a swim.' She stood up, peeled off her top, threw it to the ground and walked naked to the edge of the pool. I watched her dive in and studied her for several lengths before walking back up towards the house.

The diminutive housekeeper beckoned me into the kitchen. 'Mr Raphael back. He see you now.'

Hardly had the words stumbled from her mouth when Barry Raphael came through the door. He wore a sweaty T-shirt advertising the '84 London Marathon, navy Reebok running shorts and Asics Gel running shoes. A man in his late forties, he appeared in remarkable shape; only Raphael's lack of height let him down. He stood no higher than five feet six inches, but what few inches he had were well-muscled. His full head of hair had obviously been dyed that horrid shade of Orang Utan brown favoured by showbiz stars.

He stretched out the wrist not carrying the five-grand Rolex and shook my hand. The Filipino must have told him I was a cop. I saw no reason to say otherwise.

'Barry Raphael. Nice to meet you,' he smiled. Perfect teeth.

'Jack Mayo,' I replied.

'You with CID at Lichfield?' he asked.

'No.' I decided to come clean. 'I'm a private detective.'

The smile disappeared from his ruggedly handsome face. 'What the fuck are you doing here?' He grabbed my collar. It's always the little guys who are aggressive, don't you find?

'I was collecting for the Worldwide Fund for Nature. It's still not too late to make a donation.' I saw no point in asking him about the events in his gym. He seemed in a poor mood.

'You been questioning Beverley?' he grunted, tightening his grip.

'Not really. I spent a few minutes mentally dressing her, that's all.' I'd gotten fed up with this by now so I introduced my right knee to Raphael's reproductive organs and watched him dissolve to the floor. Then I tucked my card into his running socks and left.

It was nearly six p.m. so I called it a day and drove towards home. I remembered that Tess wanted an update but I decided that could wait till later – I'd see her at the pub. Something about this whole case stank, and for a change it wasn't Ralph.

CHAPTER 5

Alison prepared a meal for me while I phoned the office and spoke to Ralph. He'd met up with Terry Smith at a crackin' little pub in a village just a couple of miles outside Bridgnorth in the rolling Shropshire countryside.

I told Ralph I was going to the Viking pub later to see Tess, and he decided to come over and join me. We arranged to meet in the pub car park at eight o'clock. It was my round, according to him. I put the phone down and looked at my wife. I wondered why we ever got married. Or stayed together. If it wasn't for the kids we'd probably get a divorce. We don't have anything in common any more – perhaps we never did. Ruskin had a better sex life than me.

Ralph was ten minutes late, which was unusual for him. He's normally the sort of bloke to keep you waiting at least twenty minutes. His tan leather jacket was smart enough to make me think it probably fell off the back of a tourist. He'd Brylcremed his hair and taken the trouble to shave. I was wearing a brown polo shirt and natural chinos. The pub was busy for a midweek night, with standing room only in the lounge. I ordered two pints of bitter and asked the chap behind the bar if Tess was in. He looked at me as though I was stupid, so I tried the name 'Theresa'.

'She's on at closing time. Tickets are a fiver. There's a few left. You ain't Old Bill, are you?'

'No, we're not the police. Let me have two tickets.' I handed the barman fifteen quid for two tickets and the drinks. He gave me my change and two raffle tickets, numbers 46 and 47.

'Hang onto your tickets. You might win the prize later,' he added, before rushing off to serve a youth who was probably eagerly awaiting his eighteenth birthday . . . in three years' time.

I handed Ralph his pint and watched as he downed it in one and wiped the excess from around his mouth on his jacket cuffs.

'I asked the barman about Tess. She starts work at closing time and whatever she does isn't legal. I had to buy two tickets. You owe me a fiver, Ralph,' I said.

'She's working as a stripper, Jack. I've been to these do's before. Usually they draw a winning ticket and the punter gets his leg over with the bird.'

I was saddened to think of Tess having to parade naked in front of these leering men. Then that thought was ejected from my mind by two big, burly thoughts of Tess in the buff and Tess performing sex acts. My morals needed polishing up. Later.

Ralph ordered two more drinks and started to tell me of his visit to Terry Smith.

'Smith has a good memory. He even remembered dates from the sixties and seventies. According to him, Barry and Mick Raphael ran a number of seedy clubs in Birmingham, from snooker clubs to strip joints, cabaret to disco. Mostly they were in the Small Heath and Bordesley districts, never the city centre. From about 1960 they ran a protection racket which netted them each a fortune, preying on legitimate businesses and taking a percentage of any blaggings that got done on their manor. Mick, the elder of

60

the two, was the brains behind it. Barry was the younger, wilder one who enjoyed the violence, shagging and violent shagging. He was the one screwing the wife of a senior cop. By all accounts, he was a real smoothy, good-looking, and with a nice line of patter and enough ready cash to charm the pants off any bird he wanted.'

'Why did they go legit?' I asked.

'They made enough dosh to make it pointless to carry on taking risks to get their dough. In 1980 the Raphaels sold up and moved into retirement. Mick's health ain't too good after a life of sticking his dick in places it shouldn't have gone. Terry even suggested he might have got AIDS. Barry spends his time in the pursuit of his lost youth, which is why he bought the gym in Lichfield. Mick is apparently in search of *his* lost youth . . . but the name of the youth isn't known.'

Ralph could be quite witty when he liked.

'Did they ever get caught and prosecuted?' I asked.

'In the early days they both got done. Mick served two years for a nasty wounding when he sliced off the ear of some club-owner who refused to pay protection money. The Van Gogh lookalike went to the police. He wasn't seen again after the trial, mind, back in '62. Rumour is that the Raphaels used him as a binding agent in the concrete foundations of the Rotunda. Barry got done for a vicious asault on his first wife, about a week after their baby was born, in the late sixties. She pressed charges, he went inside for nine months. In the meantime they split up. The brothers were responsible for much of the violence around at that time. Both of them believed in an eye for an eye and a tooth for a tooth. In those days, apparently, Birmingham was knee-deep in guide dogs and Steradent.'

'We could do with speaking to his first wife. I wonder where she lives now. What happened to their nipper?' I asked.

'No idea,' Ralph said, draining his second pint while I

was just halfway down my first, 'but she didn't stay with Daddy.'

I ordered my partner another beer and a bag of dry roasted peanuts. He likes to throw them in the air and catch them in his mouth. As a matter of interest, he does that with much of his food.

'How did you get on today, Jack?'

'I met Michelle's step-brother, the low-life Darren Tonks. The kid lives on a diet of takeaways and contact adhesive. All he could say was that Michelle had kipped at his drum for one night only and it was the first time he'd seen her in yonks. Then we went to the gym. You'd have loved it, Ralph. I haven't seen so many women in the nude since I took a beach holiday in Yugoslavia. Everywhere you looked there were women disrobing, getting in the shower, getting out, climbing in the jacuzzi, climbing out.'

'Did you find out anything?' Ralph asked jealously, through a mouthful of chewed nuts.

'Only that the staff there are very reluctant to talk – so I went across to Barry Raphael's place. He was out pounding the pavements in his Reeboks, but Beverley Calvert was there. Boy, was she there! Ralph, it must be the friggin' weather but I went down to the pool and there was Beverley stretched out as nature intended. Jesus, what a body. You should have been there . . . Anyway, she just confirmed what was in her statement – that Paul was infatuated with Michelle and was determined to bed her, regardless of the consequences. She also said Paul's version of the events couldn't possibly be true, as Michelle was a lesbian.'

'This case reminds me of the streets of Pamplona, Jack. It's full of bullshit.' Ralph ordered more beer. We continued drinking and I even plucked up courage to ask Ralph about the incident for which he got sacked.

'I nicked a bloke for using a stolen credit card at W. H. Smith. When I got outside into Corporation Street he pulled a shiv on me, so I decked the bastard and threw his remains into the rear of the police car. The following Monday I got called into the Chief Inspector's office. I thought he was gonna praise the way I'd handled the armed man. Instead of that he said he'd watched the incident on the CCTV video recording in the controller's office and that I had used excessive force and I was a disgrace to the Queen's uniform. This fucking pencil-neck with desk-sores had the dog's bollocks to call me a disgrace. I let it ride but, on the way out of his office, something inside of me snapped. I walked back to him, picked him up by his oversized collar and planted a five-knuckle imprint on his left cheek. Last I saw of the turd, he was lying in a crumpled heap in his pending tray. I got the sack, Jack, but let me tell you something: it was bloody well worth it.'

I laughed. We often discussed the job – the police – and the way it was going. Everyone agreed that the Police and Criminal Evidence Act had turned out to be a criminal's charter. You make an arrest for a criminal offence these days, and you'd better write off the next ten hours for the associated paperwork. We were better off out of it.

Before we knew it, it was chucking-out time. Those with tickets stayed behind as the gaffer locked the doors and drew all the curtains. The chairs were arranged around the lounge to give a floorspace in the centre. The drink continued to flow and there were still forty or fifty blokes inside. And half a dozen women. After a while, a middle-aged guy with sandy-coloured hair and a blue-checked shirt clapped his hands and, in a raised voice, said, 'Gentlemen, and ladies, please give a big Viking welcome to our favourite girl . . . *Theresa!*'

There was applause and catcalls from the more common, including Ralph. We stayed over by the bar, in the corner of the room. Punters were stood, or sat four-deep around the clear area. A solitary seat had been left in the clearing. I clung to the belief that maybe Tess had a ventriloquist act. Suddenly, the curtain across a door into the pub's private area pulled back. Some rauchy music began to play and Tess stepped into the centre of the room.

She was confident, she was cocky. She'd done this before. She was dressed as a Woman Police Constable, apart from the high-heeled black shoes. Moving to the centre of the room she stopped, grinned, tossed her head to one side and removed her black leather gloves, slowly, pulling the individual fingers away before dropping them on the floor. The room was noisy. Men were whistling, shouting and giving encouragement like, 'Get 'em off' and, 'You can arrest me any day, love.'

Tess then removed her black and white checkered hat and shook her hair loose. She began slowly unbuttoning her short black tunic which bore the collar numbers '69' and slid it off her shoulders in teasing fashion. The checkered cravat followed, then the black epaulettes. Slowly she unbuttoned her white blouse, revealing, little by little, a lacy white bra. I looked at Ralph. He was almost cross-eyed with desire. Then I glanced around the room at the faces of the audience. Tess held everyone's attention with her strip. I noticed one man in particular. It was the smaller of the two guys who had showered me in accelerant back at the office. He appeared to be alone – this time, the guy built like the Arc de Triomphe wasn't with him. The thug wore the same studded-leather jacket and turned-up jeans as before, and looked about as attractive as a bag lady's tampon.

Tess had tossed her blouse aside and was wriggling out of her zip-up black skirt, revealing a tiny pair of white briefs, a suspender belt and black stockings. Ralph had even put down his pint to watch. Tess sat on the chair, pulled off her shoes, unclipped her sussies, as Ralph called them, and peeled off her stockings, slowly and seductively. She ran her tongue suggestively around her glossy lips before standing up and unclipping her belt. She reached behind her back and released her bra, and then removed it and covered her breasts with one quick, practised movement. Tess dropped the bra and placed a hand over each breast. Then, in an instant, we were looking at two nipple-tassels in blotting-paper green. She began moving her breasts in such a way that the tassels spun like the propellers on a Spitfire. At the same time she let her panties drop to the ground, exposing a G-string in the same shade of green. Tess's body was every bit as stunning as I'd imagined it would be – although I'd never imagined viewing it with fifty other guys. Her milky white breasts were large, but in proportion to the rest of her body. She had nicely shaped legs and a flat stomach. I was in love.

Tess sat on the lap of an Asian guy in the front row and invited him to remove a tassel. The Asian thought his luck had changed and he pulled the tassel off with his teeth, exhibiting Tess's light pink nipple to the crowd. Tess moved off into the audience and bent over another guy, who pulled off the other tassel while the youth alongside him put his grubby little hand on her buttocks. Tess returned to the clearing, her wondrous breasts now free to move at will. Now for the finale. Disappointingly, I thought, she moved to the little man in the black leather jacket – the one who had tried to flambé me in my office. Tess motioned to him to use his teeth to remove her G-string. The shit grinned those awful decayed pear drops and knelt before Tess, taking the string between his teeth and hauling the garment towards the floor. There were cheers and whistles as Tess Johnson's mound of tightly curled dark brown pubic hair saw daylight. She continued to gyrate, nude, for a couple of minutes before disappearing back through the curtain. There was generous applause and a long line of customers, for both the bar and the bogs. I kept my eye on the retard with the bad teeth, and saw him slip Tess's G-string into his pocket. He hadn't spotted me.

65

Ralph handed me another pint. 'That's some body our secretary's got, Jack. I wouldn't mind turking that myself.' He made a rude gesture with his thrusting hips and bumped into the youth standing next to him, causing the lad's pint to spill. The youth turned around, saw the size of Ralph and thought better about complaining.

'She's also our client, Ralph. The first rule of private detection is "don't pork your client". The second rule is "if you do pork her, keep it to yourself but don't give a discount".'

The sandy-haired guy came onto the floor again and clapped his hands. 'Once again, gents, a big hand for *Theresa!*'

The music sprang into life with a Donna Summer number and Tess emerged dressed in a multi-coloured pareu and carrying a beach mat and a bottle of suntan oil. She laid the mat on the floor and untied the pareu, letting it drop and leaving her standing in just a purple bikini with tie-sides. Tess handed the sun oil to a coloured guy with an Errol Flynn moustache and probably Errol Flynn's wedding tackle, led him to the floor and stood, statue-like, as he began rubbing the oil into her body. The music stopped and the room went quite silent as the black man gently massaged the citrus-smelling oil into Tess's exposed curves. He started on her shoulders, moved to her arms, back, tummy, thighs and, finally, her calves. Then he handed her the bottle.

'But you haven't finished yet,' Tess said. 'I want an *all-over* tan.'

The black guy grinned and undid the bow on her bra and yanked it off. She still stood rigid as he unfastened the sides of her bikini pants and let them fall. He poured oil onto his hands and rubbed it into her breasts. Her nipples appeared hard with desire as the black guy fondled her. Then he rubbed oil on her buttocks, letting his fingers slip between her legs, and the look on Tess's face said it all: she was being

66

turned on. The man oiled the tops of her thighs, then the insides between her legs, from the front this time. Tess stood rigidly, as if testing herself before taking the bottle and pouring the entire remains over her breasts. She sat on the lap of the short-arse with the bad teeth while he copped a feel of her breasts and, in return, got his clothes covered in Bergasol. It was probably the best he'd smelt all week.

Tess finished her act and exited through the curtains. The sandy-haired MC appeared and announced the winning raffle ticket as being number fifty. There were groans of disappointment around the room until it was discovered that the winner was the well-muscled, shaven-headed young man stood near to the juke-box. He wore the posey ripped T-shirt of a bodybuilder and lilac shell-suit trousers. He appeared to be a popular choice: apparently, he was the licensee's son.

'That bloke over there, Ralph,' I said, indicating Pear Drop, 'is one of the two who beat me up.'

'We'll see him outside,' Ralph promised.

'Better still,' I said, 'we'll follow him home, see where he goes.'

'Yeah, better still. We'll drop him on his own turf like he did to you,' Ralph added, his stomach rumbling like the San Andreas Fault, 'then we'll go for a curry.' Ralph had moved onto the shorts now, drinking neat whiskies. It looked like he'd be spending the night at my place. Alison would be chuffed.

The MC walked out again.

'For the last time tonight, gents, a nice big hand, and hopefully a nice big prick, for Theresa. Come on, let's hear it!'

There was rapturous applause and more whistling than you'd get at a Roger Whittaker concert. The curtain drew back as the music got switched on. Tess emerged dressed as a high-powered businesswoman, wearing her hair up in a bun, a classic navy-blue blazer, white cotton blouse, button-through skirt in a sort of khaki colour and slip-on brown shoes. To create the proper effect she had on tortoiseshell specs and carried a briefcase and a rolled-up newspaper. The muscular guy walked onto the floor as Tess sat demurely on the chair, reading the paper. The muscle-man looked around and then pulled out a large object from his pocket. It was the handle of a flick-knife. He walked up to Tess and pressed the release button and held the blade at her throat.

Ralph started to move towards them. I held him back.

'It's all part of an act, Ralph,' I said. At least, I hoped it was.

The muscle-man put the knife to Tess's throat in such a way that it made you wonder. Tess stood up, dropping the newspaper. She put up her hands in mock fear as Muscle-head told her to disrobe. She kicked off her shoes and took off her blazer. Her face was pleading for her 'attacker' to let her go. No such luck. The knife went back to her throat and the male part of the act ripped open her blouse and slapped her face. Tess fell to the ground in an obviously rehearsed way. She slowly got up and finished undressing. The blouse was removed, the skirt unbuttoned and left on the chair. Just her mauve bra and panties to go now. Again she pleaded with her assailant, whilst trying to cover her modesty with her arms. Mr Muscle approached her now, putting the knife down. He grabbed her spectacles and threw them away. He pushed Tess to her knees while he himself began to undress. His T-shirt was tossed aside, revealing a tanned, muscular torso and various tattoos. He slipped out of his trousers and was now stood before Tess, naked. His penis was excited and he pulled Tess's head towards his groin. The crowd watched with bated breath or, more likely, masturbated breath, as Tess began to indulge in oral sex. Her hands cupped the partner's testicles

68

as she ran her tongue around his dick. She stood up, took off her bra and panties, and went back to what she'd been doing. This part was for real and no mistake. Tess lay back on the floor and parted her legs. The big man climbed between them and they began copulating, in time to the music. He kissed her breasts, held her nipples between his teeth, and thrust himself deep inside the woman who had earlier made my coffee. The show ended with a round of orgasmic sighs, either real or simulated, before the muscle-man rolled off her. He got up and left the stage. Tess lay there for a short while, naked and sweaty. I compared her hourglass figure with Alison's, which had long since run to ninety minutes. Finally, Tess got up, took a bow and left the room to cheers and yells of delight. The entertainment was over, and the patrons began to drift away into the night.

Ralph and I were amongst the first to leave. We waited in a darkened doorway for the oily thug, but he took ages to come out. We both agreed he'd been to the gents for a five-knuckle shuffle. He didn't look the sort of guy who'd have a girl of his own – at least, not one you didn't need to pump air into.

At last he staggered out. He was pissed and walked with the equilibrium of Gerald Ford. We watched him get into an old Vauxhall Chevette, handpainted in smoked-haddock yellow with a boot-lid in contrasting Tabasco Sauce red. Cars are one of the few things in life which lose value when handpainted.

We got into Ralph's Allegro, the colour of which exactly matched my bathroom suite. Ralph was in no condition to drive after what he'd just consumed and he hadn't even found his car keys by the time the Chevette roared off towards Burntwood. Eventually, though, he fired the car into life and we took off after Chummy. The Chevette turned right at Swan Island, towards Lichfield. Ralph went continental and took us anti-clockwise around the island.

The Chevette pulled into a 24-hour garage for petrol. We waited until it moved off from the forecourt and headed back up towards Sankey's Corner along Cannock Road. Both cars struggled to get up the hill. Ralph nipped through a red light at Spring Hill Road in order to stay close to the Vauxhall. We followed right on to Rugeley Road and right again towards Boney Hay.

'Either he knows he's being tailed or he's got a piss-poor sense of direction,' said Ralph helpfully.

Finally the Chevette pulled onto a dirt track leading into a field in which stood a dilapidated caravan. Perhaps a two-berth, this wasn't just old – it was the prototype. The thug parked his car in a careless fashion and unlocked the caravan door. He went in and a light came on.

'He lives worse than I do,' snorted Ralph. 'Let's go and have a few words. He looks in need of company.'

Ralph rapped on the caravan door, while I stayed in the shadows.

The door opened and the little guy stood there in his patterned boxer shorts. 'Yeah?' he asked.

Ralph, a man of few words at times like these, hit him with a blow not dissimilar to that of the meteorite thudding into Siberia, a blow that caused Chummy to hit the far caravan wall and start it rocking. Ralph went inside. I followed. It was as though the place had been decorated by Hurricane Annie. There was rubbish everywhere. Clothes were dumped on the floor, old newspapers gathered dust, empty beer cans fought for floorspace with porn magazines. Terry Waite lived in better conditions, I'm sure, back in Beirut.

We waited for Norman Paget to come round. We found his name on various driving and other documents. He was only a provisional licence holder, naughty boy. I wondered why he had chequebooks and credit cards in other names, including one Mrs I. Rafique. Ralph took a leak on Paget's bed, to save having to trek outside. Lucky for Paget, I thought, that Ralph hadn't yet had his curry.

Paget came to, like someone at the dentist's after taking gas, and sat up holding his jaw.

'How's your bad mouth, pal?' asked Ralph.

'You've broken my fuckin' jaw,' Paget said, through clenched teeth.

'We're here to ask you some questions on your specialist subject, Mr Paget – crime. You have sixty seconds starting from . . . now. Who sent you to threaten me?' I asked.

'Go fuck yourself.'

'I'm sorry, that's the wrong answer. You must pay a forfeit.'

Ralph stamped on the fingers of his left hand, pinning them to the floor. Paget screamed in pain.

'You can't do this. I got rights,' he squealed, holding his hand and his jaw, best he could.

'You could make things easy for yourself, Norman. Just tell us what we want to know,' I said, understandingly.

Ralph put Paget into a Home Office approved restraint hold and we watched the guy burst through the pain threshold. 'Okay, okay. I'll talk. Just let me go.'

Ralph kept the hold on. 'Who sent you to my office?'

'English . . . *aaargh*! Eddie English.'

'Why?' I mused.

'I'm the paid help. He didn't say.'

'Who pays your wages, then?' I asked.

'Mr Raphael usually. I'm freelance.'

'A freelance thug – that's nice. I bet the Government paid you forty quid a week on the Enterprise Allowance to start up. Am I right, Norm baby?'

He was too anguished to reply.

'Got anywhere you can stay tonight, pal?' asked Ralph.
'Why?'

' 'Cos we're torching this place. It's a fuckin' health risk.'

'You can't do that.'

'Yes, we can. It's democracy at work. The two of us outvoted the one of you. Let me just add this, Norman. You're in the wrong line of business, you really are. I don't ever want to see you again 'cos, like, if I do,' at this point Ralph put more pressure on Paget's skinny wrist, 'I'll take you up Cannock Chase and provide you with cheap accommodation in the form of a shallow grave. You understand?'

Paget nodded as best he could. Ralph let him go and the lower-life fell to the floor. Ralph went out to his car and returned with a plastic petrol container in pollutant red. He splashed four-star across the insides of the caravan, saving just one porn magazine for himself. Then he dragged Paget outside and tossed a match into the van, pulling the door shut. Flames quickly roared through the caravan. For good measure, Ralph scattered the remaining petrol into Paget's Chevette and torched that, too.

Paget was sitting on the grass nearby, holding his face. He was wearing just his cute boxer shorts.

'Burn well, Vauxhalls,' Ralph stated. 'Should have brought some jacket potatoes along.'

We watched for a short time before deciding to make ourselves scarce before the fire brigade and police turned up. The field was brightly illuminated by the flames leaping from the two wrecked vehicles.

As we slowly drove out of the field, Ralph wound down his car window and shouted across to Paget.

'Can we offer you a lift anywhere, Norman?'

CHAPTER 6

Ralph had dropped me off at the Viking to pick up my car before driving back to Birmingham. He decided against staying the night on the basis that he would still be able to get a Balti at Srinegar Mo's. I was relieved. So would Alison have been if she'd known. Ralph and I also agreed not to say anything to Tess about her performance at the pub. It was none of our business how she made her living and we didn't want to embarrass the girl, though how you could embarrass somebody who performs sex in front of an audience of fifty men was something I hadn't really considered.

I slept on the sofa rather than wake the missus, and next morning I was out of the house before she or the kids were even awake. It was seven-thirty when I pulled onto Tess's driveway. I knocked on her door and watched her approach through the frosted glass. She opened the door wearing only a towel. Her hair and skin were wet.

'Sorry Jack, I was in the shower. Come on in. You're early.'

I went inside and watched her shut the front door. She wasn't wearing the towel – she was holding it in front of her. The whole of her back was exposed and I observed drops of water trickle down her spine and into the cleft between her buttocks. She turned back to face me.

'Go into the kitchen and make yourself a cuppa. I'll be

down in two minutes.' She ran upstairs, leaving soggy footprints on the plain green carpet.

I took to the kitchen and switched on the jug kettle which matched the beige of the fitted cupboards. There was the policewoman's hat on the pine table, next to the local free newspaper, the *Lichfield Mercury*. The headline said something about a Northern Relief Road about to scythe through the district, and page three ran a picture, fully clothed, of Lichfield's Bower Queen. The kettle boiled and I dropped tea bags into two scrupulously clean china mugs. Tess walked in just as I'd finished making the brew.

She wore a white cardigan with a deep V-neck and button front closing over a pair of white denim jeans and white sandals. The cardigan was adult enough to have a mind of its own and it emphasised the point by continuously slipping off her shoulders. Tess regularly pushed it back up again. Doubtless she was wearing nothing beneath it.

'You thinking of joining up?' I asked, pointing at the police hat.

'No,' she laughed, quickly changing the subject. 'I thought you were coming to see me last night to update me on your trip to the Raphaels?'

'Yeah, sorry. It got quite late. I spoke to Beverley Calvert, and she's sticking by her statement, that Paul came onto Michelle and she didn't want to know. Beverley also said several other things.'

'Such as?' Tess looked serious.

I decided against mentioning Paul's alleged stud-like qualities and said, 'Michelle was a lesbian.'

Tess's body looked ready to burst from the cardigan. I got ready to catch it. She was showing more of her cleavage than I could cope with at that early hour.

'Jack, I'm not coming in today. I had a late night last night, and I think I'll just spend the day getting a little sun. Is that all right with you?'

'Fine. I'll phone you later after I've spoken to Noddy Jacobs about including Paul in his workload.'

'No, come round – I'll fix a salad or something.'

'Fair enough. I'll bring a bottle of wine,' I said, gulped back the tea and left for Birmingham.

Ralph was still snoring like a warthog when I got to the office. I could hear the noise without opening his door. Potential clients arriving early would have been well impressed.

I phoned Noddy Jacobs and arranged to see him for a liquid lunch at the Queen's Head pub in Steelhouse Lane, one of the nearest bars to the Victoria Law Courts in Birmingham. Meanwhile, I thought I'd give the boy Darren Tonks another chance to get things off his chest.

When I got there, the car park at Lech Walesa House was cordoned-off by two white police Maestros with blue flashing lights. An ambulance was also in attendance. I asked one of the bobbies, a lad I knew by sight from Digbeth, what had happened.

'A jumper,' he said. I knew then that Darren was dead.

'Kid leapt from the balcony on the fifteenth floor and landed on the roof of some bloke's Rover 216. It's a Cabriolet now.'

'Not Flat sixty-one by any chance?' I asked, although I knew the answer already.

'Here, how did you know?' the cop asked.

'Intuition,' I said, and left it at that.

'He was a glue-sniffer. Probably sniffed a headful and then took his elastic-free bungee jump. What a waste of a life.' The cop walked off, hands in his pockets and a 'seen it all before' look on his face. I recognised that look. I had worn one myself for ten years. A crowd of local rubber-neckers had gathered to watch Darren's twisted remains being loaded into the blood-wagon. I drove off to town.

Darren could have committed suicide, though I doubted

it. My guess was that Darren was helped over the balcony by a person or persons unknown. Somebody was covering his tracks, and it sure as hell wasn't Paul Johnson.

A pound coin bought me a lousy one hour and fifteen minutes in one of the Birmingham City Council's pay and display bays in Colmore Row, which was as near as I could get to Steelhouse Lane. I hurried into the Queen's Head and spotted Noddy propping up the bar with his elbow perched on the wet bar towel. Noddy made Ralph look like he just fell off the cover of *GQ* magazine. Possessing a dress sense that was influenced less by Coco Chanel than Coco-the-Clown, he had a shock of white hair over a pink face and the heavily-veined nose of the seasoned boozer. He always wore a colourful bow tie and today was no exception.

'Jack,' he said, spotting me approaching. 'Nice to see you, son. How's things? How's your dear old dad?'

'He's still dead,' I answered politely, 'but thanks for asking.' I shook his hand. Dad had worked for Noddy as a 'runner', for a couple of years after he retired from the police.

'I heard you got a medical retirement?' he said, draining his gin and tonic.

'Yeah, I've got a duff knee – but it's fine in this weather. What you drinking?'

'G and T, old boy.'

'What do you want to eat?' I asked.

'I never mix food and drink, Jack, and right now I'm drinking. What did you want to see me about that's so urgent?'

I ordered his G and T and a straight tonic water for myself. 'I'm working as a private detective. Remember Ralph Grice? He's my partner.'

'God forbid!'

'Yes, well . . . Anyway, we're on a case where a young woman has hired us to find out who killed a girl called Michelle Rosa. She's particularly interested since her husband Paul is accused of the murder and he's sat in Winson Green Prison.'

'I see. Where do I come in?'

'The girl's husband is represented by Eddie English. We don't trust him, however competent he may be. We'd rather have a brief who's trustworthy, regardless of how good he is.'

'Did I miss a compliment there? I assume the accused is happy to change solicitors mid-stream, as it were?'

The drinks arrived and Jacobs ate the lemon slice in his.

'Yes, I'm certain he will. Eddie English was provided by Paul's boss, who was also the boss of the dead girl. Sounds like a conflict of interests to me.'

'Who is his boss?' Jacobs asked.

'Barry Raphael.'

'You'd better tell me the whole story, Jack. And order some more drinks.'

I outlined what I already knew of the case to Noddy and he listened carefully, in his learned fashion. Half an hour later, and after four more gin and tonics, Jacobs gave a big sigh.

'Frankly, Jack, things look in pretty poor shape for the young man. I'll take the case because I like a challenge but I'd have felt more confident representing Pol Pot.'

I handed him my file of papers which he promised to photocopy and return to me. I don't have a copier, either. Then he handed me several of his cards and rushed off, having arranged to contact me again after he'd spoken to Johnson. I sprinted back to my car and was relieved to find there was no parking ticket on it. The council tickets are very keenly priced.

It was early afternoon when I went back to the office to speak to Ralph, and I felt sure he'd be awake by now. He was. His breath required a Haz-Chem warning.

'Where you bin, Jack?' he enquired, holding his head, like it had just been set in cement on his shoulders.

'I've just been to see Noddy Jacobs.'

'Any joy?'

'He'll represent Johnson, provided the lad's agreeable. Having said that, Jacobs listened as I outlined the case details and more or less threw in the towel.'

'Either way, Jack, he's a better bet than English. Anything you want me to do today?'

'Don't you mean what's left of today? Yeah – we need some background on Michelle Rosa. I don't even know what the girl looked like. Her step-brother died this morning, by the way.'

'What happened – did he OD on a PrittStick?' Ralph was always sympathetic.

'He leapt from his balcony on the fifteenth floor like one of those Acapulco cliff divers, only he didn't land in the warm blue Pacific. He landed on a hard, metallic green Rover saloon. Turns out the car was owned by a social worker visiting somebody in the block.'

'They in the car at the time?' Ralph muttered.

'No.'

'Shame.'

Ralph has a long list of people he detests, and social workers are a permanent fixture at the top, along with senior police officers, politicians of all parties, punks, skinheads, rent boys, the idle rich, the idle poor and homosexuals.

'All I learned from the glue-sniffer was the fact that he and Michelle shared the same mother, who worked as a tom down in Balsall Heath. Maybe she used the name "Tonks". That's all I can tell you, Ralph. Plus she's white and presumably well into her forties.'

'Okay. I'll get right onto it.'

'And Ralph – no shagging on expenses.'

'What you gonna be doing?' Ralph asked, while simultaneously trying to dislodge something from between his front upper teeth with the point of a compass.

'I'm going across to update Tess and, if there's time, I'll call on English, see if he's had any more paperwork come through from CPS.'

I looked at the state of Ralph. Greasy hair, blackheads, pimples. Ralph's body produced more oil than Bahrain. He found what he was searching for with the compass and, having examined it briefly, flicked it across the room. Ralph has more ways to make me heave than anybody else I have ever met.

'What do you make of the case, Jack? I mean, to be honest, it's fuckin' complicated. I really ain't got a clue who did what to who.'

'It goes back to what we said before. Either Johnson is guilty and we're wasting our time, but getting paid for wasting our time, or he's innocent and he's been stitched. I don't believe for one minute that Tonks killed himself. He knew more than he was telling about Michelle Rosa, and somebody needed to shut his mouth. Two guys come to our office and work me over. Then we find out they're working for English, who in turn works for Barry Raphael. Raphael pays English to represent Johnson. Why? The staff at the gym won't talk about Michelle and make statements which point the finger at Johnson. Raphael owns the gym. Everything seems to revolve around that bastard.'

'Do you reckon he killed Michelle?' Ralph asked.

'It would all fit together. Raphael's not a happy man until there's pudenda on the agenda. Michelle comes to work at the gym and we can only assume she's another shapely, good-looking girl. Now, if we believe Johnson, she comes onto him and he finally succumbs to the pleasures of her flesh. Raphael, meanwhile, has plans of his own to get inside Michelle's knickers. She gives him the red light and it hurts

Barry's male pride. So he takes her to Chasewater, rips her clothes off and is about to slip her a length when he's disturbed. He panics and stabs her before making off. He's been watching her and he knows she's had sex with Johnson, so who's the perfect man to stitch with Michelle's murder. Our boy Johnson.'

'Sounds good, Jack. The use of his own brief means Raphael can control the Court case to a certain extent, as well. Where does the bit about Michelle being a lesbian come in?'

'No idea. Maybe it was just Beverley winding me up. I'll drop it on Vanessa's toes when I get the chance. When you spoke to Terry Smith, did he say where Mick Raphael was living these days?'

'He did say but I've forgotten. It was near to his brother. If you want to find him, try hanging round public toilets at midnight. Mick Raphael will be the gaunt-looking man in the pink tracksuit.'

'Is he really bent?' I asked.

'No – at least, not fully. He had a bigger libido than Barry and pulled anything that took his fancy, bird or bloke. I just think he found blokes easier to pull as he got older. He never had Barry's good looks.'

'Is he married?'

'I think so, I know Barry is. The wives stay very much in the background. Barry's missus is a bit of a corker, apparently, one of these older, sophisticated tarts who really look after their figures.'

'Any kids?' I asked.

'Nah. He had a kid by his first wife but he never got to know him or her 'cos he split up with Mum.'

'I think I'll pay Barry another visit,' I mused.

'Want me to come with you, Jack?'

'No, you crack on and find this prostitute. Maybe if we approach this thing from two sides we can squeeze out the truth.'

'That's fuckin' profound,' laughed Ralph as he walked to the door. 'If I don't see you back here later, I'll ring you at home.' He left.

I stopped at Tesco's store in Brownhills on the way across to Burntwood and bought a bottle of Frascati. I felt it would go down nicely, chilled, on such a hot day. It was four o'clock by my watch when I got to Tess's house, which meant it was three-fifty in reality, the damn watch always being ten minutes fast.

The BMW 7 series parked on her drive was familiar. The window on the passenger side was open a couple of inches; the CD was missing and the car stank of canine crap. It was Eddie English's car all right.

I got back into the Golf and drove it out of sight, around the next corner. Then I stood and waited for English to leave. It was four-thirty, real time, before he appeared at the door, bidding adieu to Tess. He was wearing the sort of cream linen suit that looks great in the tropics but always a bit iffy in the Western Midlands. When he'd reversed out of the drive and headed towards Lichfield, I moved back and parked in the street outside the house.

Tess answered the door. She was crying. 'Oh Jack, I'm so glad it's you.' She pulled the door wide open and I walked inside. She was wearing a stretchy, cotton-Lycra vest dress in the shade of orange that hurts your eyes.

'Tess, what's the matter?' I asked. Tears were streaming down her face. No wonder she always had blotchy eyes.

'It's Paul. He's told English that he intends to plead guilty to manslaughter if the prosecution will agree. He's staying in prison, Jack.'

I put my arms around her and pulled her close. I could feel she was naked under the dress. She was warm and smelled just like a woman should.

'Was it Paul's idea, or did English sow some seeds of

81

doubt in his mind?' I asked. My left hand was in the small of her back, my right hand caressing the bare flesh of her shoulders.

'English went to see Paul today. Apparently the police uncovered more evidence after another search of the gym. They found some photographs of Michelle in various stages of undress, taken at the gym, and some sadistic porn magazines – all hidden away in the locked drawer of a desk used by Paul. Eddie suggested he could plea bargain with the prosecution and get a manslaughter charge substituted for the murder one, in return for a guilty plea. Eddie told Paul that there was a good chance he could get a light sentence and be out in a couple of years. Murder meant life inside. Paul agreed. Jack, what can we do?'

'Look,' I said, trying to sound convincing, 'it doesn't change anything. If we find the real killer, nothing alters.'

'Maybe I should go along with Paul's wishes. He could be out in two years and we could start afresh in Greece.'

'That's up to you,' I said, letting my left hand slip down to her rump. 'You're the boss.'

'Jack, I'm so mixed up. Hold me, please.' She buried her face into my chest. I held her tighter and rubbed her back with my right hand. I'm not sure if it comforted her, but it did me the world of good. I don't know what came over me but I moved my right hand to her left thigh and gently massaged it, easing my way under her dress until I was caressing her hip. Then I lowered my left hand to her right thigh and did the same. I was getting turned on and Tess was starting to breathe deeply, like she was enjoying it. She didn't tell me to stop. Her dress was now up round her waist. I put both hands on her soft bum, then lifted the dress upwards and over her head in one quick movement. I was impressing the shit out of myself. Tess was now naked in my arms.

'Take me to bed, Jack,' she purred. That sounded like an invite. I picked her up under the shoulders and knees and carried her upstairs to the bedroom, where I laid her on the bed and quickly stripped off myself. I had a hard-on like a barber's pole.

I moved alongside Tess and stroked her face, her neck and thighs. I caressed those gorgeous breasts and sucked on her hard, aroused nipples. My fingers went between her legs and found her already moist and ready. I rolled between her legs and thrust my quivering penis inside her. It was warm and tight, almost uncomfortably so. We thrashed about in our sweaty embrace, probing, kissing, biting and scratching until my mind lost its battle with my body and I was unable to prevent what the criminologists call 'seed emission'. Afterwards I lay exhausted in Tess's arms while she ran her fingers up and down my back.

'You don't mess about, do you, Jack?' she eventually whispered.

'I believe in the big bang theory,' I said.

'I never meant for this to happen.' She looked worried.

'Tess, it happened. End of story. Paul will never find out.'

We lay in each other's arms. Tess had freckles on her chest. There was a small mole on her neck, otherwise her skin was clear. She sat up and leaned over me. Her breasts moved independently of each other and her body.

She smiled. 'Let's do it again, Jack. Are you man enough?' She straddled me and began trying to rub some life into the peeled grape which posed as my manhood. I was hung like a hamster but what can you do? She didn't seem to care. Tess ran her tongue up the inside of my thighs, all the time looking up at me. I just lay back and thought of English.

It was nearly eight o'clock when I woke up. Eight o'clock in the morning, that is. I'd spent the night with Tess and finally got to sleep around three. The girl was insatiable. I couldn't work her out. I woke with feelings of guilt. Guilt over her husband and guilt over my wife. I lifted Tess's right thigh off my belly and crept out of bed. I was dressed and out of the house by eight-fifteen.

I drove straight to the Raphael household. English probably wouldn't want to know me any more now that Paul was pleading guilty, so I postponed meeting him. It was still early when I reached The Old School House. I made a note of the registration numbers of the cars parked on the gravel drive – a pal of mine in the police would check them on the PNC for me later. There was a gold Mercedes, a red Mazda sports and a white Golf.

I'd been flicking through the channels on my car stereo for a couple of minutes looking for something half decent to listen to when a distinguished-looking guy in his late fifties came out of the house. He had the face of a boxer – a losing boxer. His smashed nose made him look uglier than even nature had intended. He had neatly-styled grey hair and was casually dressed in check slacks, white shoes and a Pringle sweater. I guessed this to be Mick Raphael. Contrary to rumour control, he looked perfectly healthy.

Mick got into the Mercedes and reversed out of the drive, spraying gravel everywhere. I followed him – at a discreet distance, of course, not like on these TV cop shows where the police tail a suspect by sitting in the car directly behind. The Merc sped down towards Lichfield before taking the Walsall Road. Mick turned left at the Pipehill traffic lights and then pulled onto the drive of a three-storey farmhouse on the outskirts of Wall, or 'Letocetum' as the Romans called it. The Romans had the good sense to leave before they got stuck in the traffic at Pipehill, too. The house was covered in ivy. It looked more like an old school house than Barry's place. I looked on enviously for a while before turning round and returning to Lower Longdon. The Golf had gone, and a Saab was parked in its spot.

I decided to go straight round the back of the house and

down to the pool. It was the right move. Barry Raphael was sat at the resin table talking into his portable phone. He wore a turquoise thong. Men of his age shouldn't wear thongs – it just isn't right. Beverley was frolicking in the swimming pool with Vanessa, and appeared unusually coy in that she was wearing a white running vest which had, in any case, got so wet that it was see-through. Vanessa had forgotten to bring her costume.

Raphael saw me out of the corner of his eye and finished his phone call abruptly. The girls stopped what they were doing.

'If this is a bad time just say, Barry,' I said breezily. 'Morning, ladies. Nice glutes, Vanessa.'

'Mr Mayo – I've been expecting you to return.' Raphael turned to face me. Either it was true what they said about Raphael, or somebody had hidden a two-man submarine down the front of his thong. 'Come and join us. Like a drink? I feel we got off on the wrong foot last time. Let me apologise.'

'I'll have a tonic water,' I said, surprised at Raphael's *bonhomie*, and sat down where I could get a poolside view of the girls, who began tossing a beach ball to each other.

Raphael brought me the drink and said, 'Bottoms up,' which was rather apt in the circumstances. 'What can I do for you, Mr Mayo?' he added, sitting on the edge of the pool, dangling his hairy legs in the water.

'I'd like to ask a few questions about Paul Johnson and Michelle Rosa, if that's all right with you.'

'I've got nothing to hide,' he shrugged. It rang strangely true, coming from a man in a thong.

'Firstly, why did you pay for Paul's defence brief?'

'He's an employee. Eddie English is an employee, to a certain extent. It was the least I could do.'

'Did you find Michelle attractive?'

'I find most women attractive.'

'That doesn't answer my question,' I said.

'Yes, I found her immensely attractive. Is that better?'

'Did you sleep with her?'

'You're getting personal, Mr Mayo. It's none of your business who I sleep with. However, for the record – no, I did not.'

Raphael was one of life's hairy people, with a thick covering over his torso, arms and legs. If he ever went broke he could always get a job as a gorilla-gram . . . and he wouldn't need a costume.

'I don't wanna sound pushy, Barry – can I call you Barry? – but do you know what I think? I think you killed Michelle Rosa and then cleverly set up Paul Johnson as the patsy.'

'You should stick to serving process, Mayo. You're way out of your depth.' He turned towards the house and shouted, 'Errol! . . . I think you should go now,' he added.

I looked towards the house and saw the black body-builder from the Amazon Gym walking down the path. He looked like he meant business.

'Errol, show Mr Mayo the exit,' Raphael said. I think the girls sensed trouble and climbed out of the pool. I was right about Vanessa – she *had* shaved off her pubic hair. Errol came up close and grinned. He had half a dozen gold teeth.

'So that's where the Brink's Mat gold got hidden,' I said by way of a joke. On the basis that attack is the best form of defence, I took Errol's right wrist and swung him quickly round. He lost his balance and took to the pool. Archimedes' principle was proved again.

'Girls,' Raphael shouted. 'Errol can't swim!'

The two girls jumped back into the pool and salvaged what they could of big Errol.

I began to saunter off, turning just once to shout back at Raphael, 'You'll be very popular in prison in that thong, Raphael. It'll be great for male bonding.' I grinned, but I was grinning prematurely. Right in front of me on the path stood the giant from my office, looking as if he was in a foul mood.

I tried the attack-is-the-best-form-of-defence ploy again and punched him hard in his stomach. It was like hitting a bag of wet sand. I saw his right fist heading towards me like a demolition ball, then day became night as I dropped to the ground.

CHAPTER 7

I didn't expect to wake up again, other than as part of some concrete structure somewhere, but maybe Raphael was getting soft in his old age. As it happened, I woke up lying in six inches of water in what turned out to be Redmoor Brook, on the edge of Gentleshaw Common. I'd received a thorough working over and my ribs were giving me gip. Still, I was in one piece and alive.

I hobbled to the road and realised where I was. As it was nearer to Tess's place than mine, I made it the half-mile or so to the house. She opened the door and looked at me like I was selling pegs.

'Jack! What happened?'

'I got struck by a chunk of Skylab,' I said.

She led me upstairs and switched on the shower, then helped me out of my clothes and pushed me under the warm water. Within half an hour I'd started to feel a little better. I wrapped a towel round my waist and went downstairs. Tess had fixed me a long, cool drink of something roughly the same colour as the dress I'd pulled off her the previous night. For the record, today she was wearing a pretty floral belted dress which was, I think, the most I'd ever seen her body covered.

'I went to see Paul this morning, Jack. He's still intent on pleading guilty to manslaughter. Do you think he could be got at in prison?'

'If the IRA can smuggle a gun into Brixton inside a training shoe, then I'm sure somebody could get a message to Paul.'

'He just didn't seem the same man I know – he was really down and depressed. He worries me. Can we go for a walk, Jack? I feel like I need some fresh air in my lungs. We can take the wine you brought yesterday, and I've made some sandwiches. Please say yes.'

'Yeah, but I can't move too fast. Remember that.'

She sorted out the food and drink while I went upstairs to dress. When I returned, I found her sat at the driver's wheel of her Mini. It wasn't easy to get into a small car in my condition.

Tess drove us to Chasewater, where she parked near the Chasetown High School. I followed her down Pool Road and through Vietnam-like undergrowth to the walled-end of the pool. Although it was a weekday, plenty of people had found time to relax there, either in boats on the water or on the banks. Tess led me anti-clockwise around the shoreline. If it wasn't for the electricity pylons in the distance, you could almost be at the seaside. The sun's rays reflected off the vast stretch of water and I felt glad to be alive. Tess led me beyond the sailing club to an area of pebble beach on the north shore, overlooked by thick undergrowth and trees. We sat down. I opened the wine and we drank from paper cups.

It was a nice, secluded spot. A man walking his little dog, which looked like a rat with a perm, was the only person to pass us.

'Paul told me to sell up and move to Greece,' Tess said quietly, 'and that he'd join me when he was released. He promised the time would just fly by. I'm really confused now, Jack. I don't even know whether I believe he's innocent any more. He admitted that he slept with Michelle on the night of the murder.'

'I know. He told me.' I lay back and closed my eyes.

'Maybe he did kill her – I just don't know,' she whispered.

It went quiet for a few minutes and I cat-napped. When I looked up, Tess was gone. Her dress hung on the tree behind where we sat.

'Come and join me, Jack!' she shouted.

I looked straight ahead and saw Tess paddling in the water, in her underwear.

'Come on in, the water's lovely! Refreshing, and cool.' She was wearing those loose-fitting French knickers, in white, and a white bra.

I shook my head and smiled. Tess waded further out and then submerged herself in the water up to her neck. When she stood up, her knickers were moulded to her form. By this time the old guy with his dog was on his way back. He stood and watched. Tess saw him watching and submerged herself again. She was down for a few seconds before again standing up, this time entirely naked, her undergarments in her hand. She stood rinsing herself in the water for a while, paying particular attention to her breasts, before wading back to the shore. The old guy appeared to be in a state of shock. Tess wrung out her bra and pants, hung them on the same tree as her dress, then lay down nude on the pebbles, near me.

'Tess, you can't bathe like that here,' I hissed. 'This is Staffordshire. You'll have people complaining.'

The old man eventually carried on walking, but not before his eyes had combed every inch of Tess's nubile body.

'Don't be such a prude, Jack. Anyway, it's just too hot for clothes.' She closed her eyes. I finished what was left of the wine and watched the speedboats in the distance. Then I fell asleep.

Tess woke me with a gentle dig in the ribs which caused me to flinch.

'Sorry,' she said, 'I forgot you're sore there. It's time we headed back.' She still hadn't dressed. She picked up her clothes and began walking off along the shore, like she was on a secluded beach in the Algarve or somewhere.

'Tess, for God's sake – put your dress on!' I said, but my words fell on deaf ears. I hurried to catch her up. She dropped her clothes and continued to walk. I picked them up. 'Tess!'

We were close to the sailing club now – but it didn't bother her in the least. The girl was an exhibitionist of the highest order. Half a dozen people in wetsuits stopped what they were doing and watched the shapely girl stroll past without a stitch on. Further down the beach, towards Pool Road, two teenage boys with fishing rods stared goggle-eyed at Tess. Back at the Mini, she got into the driver's seat and prepared to drive off, still nude.

I got in beside her. 'Fair enough, Tess. You've had your fun,' I said.

'This isn't fun, Jack. This is what I do for a living. I'm a stripper. I take my clothes off and men pay to ogle my body. Well, today they got a freebie – so what?'

'You told me you were a temp,' I reminded her.

She laughed. 'I wanted to sound respectable. Stripping falls in the same category as wheel-clamping, timeshare sales and,' she paused, '*private investigation.*'

Then she switched on the ignition and accelerated away, turning left into Chasetown High Street. I hid my face as she stopped at the zebra crossing. Further up the High Street we got stuck in the nightly queue of traffic in the rush hour, at Sankey's Corner.

Passers-by whistled when they saw Tess's state of un-dress. Motorists sounded their horns: one guy in a Metro went up the kerb and narrowly missed a lamp-post. I was relieved to get back to her house. Luckily, none of her neighbours appeared to be about as she got out of the car and walked to her front door.

'I'll see you tomorrow,' I said, heading for my Golf.

'Must you go?' she said.

'Yeah. I promised I'd see Ralph.'

I was having a conversation with a nude woman in the middle of the street. I got into the VW and made off quickly towards Brum. Tess was proving to be as enigmatic as the rest of case. I needed to talk to somebody normal. *Like Ralph.*

Ralph was sat at his desk when I got back, tucking into a doner kebab and chips. His diet leaves a lot to be desired – such as protein, vitamins and essential carbohydrates. His habit is to shove as much food as possible into his mouth and then try to hold a normal conversation. This results in morsels of food flying everywhere. Ralph was also smelling like a wino's armpit.

'How did you get on, Jack?' he asked, as I dodged a piece of well-chewed gristle.

'I met the big ugly git who worked me over and he worked me over again to prove it hadn't been a fluke. Apart from that I dropped it on Raphael's toes that he killed Michelle.'

'How did he take it?' Ralph asked, sucking his fingers.

'Badly, as you can imagine. Apart from that, Ralph, it's been the usual round of naked women, wine and song. How was your day in the red-light district?'

'I met a coloured bird selling her twat just off Balsall Heath Road. I greased her palm with a tenner and she told me where I could find a scabby old pro called Maggie Tonks.'

'You certain it was her palm you greased, Ralph?' I asked.

'If you'd seen her you wouldn't ask that question. Anyhow, this Maggie Tonks bird lives in a maisonette in Highgate. I went round about an hour ago but there was nobody in. I thought we could try again later.'

'Do you think it's the woman we're looking for?' I asked.

'No. But she's as close as I got.'

'We'll go round and speak to her. You might get the chance to grease *her* palm too, Ralphie. I'll buy you an evening of thrills with her as a bonus.'

'You're on,' said Ralph. And he wasn't joking.

Ralph took us in his Allegro, which didn't look out of keeping in the down-market area. It was eight o'clock when we arrived in Mendip Grove, a little cul de sac surrounded by four-storey maisonettes. The Grove was crammed with cars, and scores of West Indian youths were milling about. The constant thud of reggae told us both why; there was a blues party taking place in one of the upper maisonettes. Rastafarians leaned over the balcony of the communal walkway, drinking Red Stripe. The smell of ganja hung in the air and I longed to be back on the shores of Chasewater with a naked girl.

Ralph parked on the footpath out of habit and we began looking for number 28. Luckily it was on the ground floor opposite the blues party. Ralph pressed the white doorbell and it dropped off the wall. I knocked on the door. No response. Ralph kicked the door. It opened as far as the security chain would allow, and a woman peered out.

'Maggie Tonks?' I said, sounding too much like a cop for my own liking.

'What do you want?' she replied.

'We're private detectives. Can we speak to you about Darren and Michelle?' I asked.

'They've gone and pegged it, duck,' Ralph grunted. He was a great bloke to be with when you had to break the news of a death. He once knocked on the door of Mr Davidson's wife to inform her that her husband had been killed in a pile-up on the M6, and addressed her as 'Widow Davidson' right from the off.

'What?' Maggie Tonks said.

'I'm afraid they're both dead,' I said, looking daggers at Ralph. Maggie slid the chain off the door and let us in.

She was in better shape than I'd imagined, although her eyes had the wide stare of somebody who's soaked their contact lenses overnight in ammonia, her hair was that unnatural dark red that comes in a bottle, and her face had a little too much make-up on it to hide the lines of age. She wore cheap costume jewellery on any part of the body that jewellers had a monopoly on, and some they hadn't: big plastic earrings, about a dozen bangles on each wrist, half a dozen neck chains and rings on every finger. She had on a black chiffon housecoat over a black satin camisole which displayed too much of her cleavage. Her skin had the wrinkled, liver-spotty look of a woman in her fifties and her large bust had sagged over the years. She didn't need a bra; she needed a belt with a D-cup. Her black satin skirt had a slit up the side, revealing acres of puffy, cream cellulite. She wore those awful high-heeled slippers with the fluffy pom-pom on the front. If she went on *What's my line?* you'd never have guessed she was a prostitute – I don't think.

She poured herself a large gin. I got ready to refuse a drink but the offer never came.

'Both my babies are dead,' she mumbled.

'Yes. And we have reason to believe both were murdered,' I said.

'Murdered? I can't believe I'm hearing this. Michelle as well?' She drained the glass and refilled it. 'I always knew Darren would come to no good, but Michelle had a proper job down in London. What happened?'

'She was killed by a colleague in a sex attack while working at a gym over in Lichfield.' I tried to sound sympathetic. 'Who is Michelle's father, Maggie?' I asked.

She knocked back another drink and looked at me, then at Ralph. My partner had lit up a cheap Panatella and was filling the room with white smoke and bad smells.

94

'Barry Raphael,' she said, and you could have knocked me down with a Fetherlite.

'Fuckin' hell,' gasped Ralph. 'I didn't expect that!'

'I was Barry's wife. We married in 1966, just after England won the World Cup, and Michelle was born two years later. I was a dancer at their cabaret club.'

'Dancer?' Ralph thought aloud.

'Dancer, stripper, call it what you like. Barry was never a one-woman man – he always liked to dip his quill in other people's inkwells. In the same year Michelle was born, he ditched me for some other bimbo. Barry's sex-mad. I always thought he had a pacemaker fitted to his cock.'

'Who was Darren's father?' I asked.

'Micky Raphael. Talk about keep it in the family, eh? He comforted me after the break-up with Barry. Mind you, his idea of comforting me included having me dress as Barbarella.'

'So you got a child by each brother. How come you turned to prostitution?' I asked.

'Because they dumped me. I was an embarrassment, so I got work the only way I could. I had a good body in those days and I worked the hotels but I drank too much and now I'm stuck in this god-forsaken shit-tip.' The sound of Bob Wailer and the Marleys in the background, echoing through the block, emphasised her point.

While Ralph stayed to fill Maggie in on the details, or just to fill her in, I walked to nearby Hurst Street and took a black cab back to the office. I needed peace and quiet to think.

I didn't get it. On arriving back at corporate HQ, I found another of Tess's handwritten notes pinned to the doorframe. It was to the point: *In café, please come. Tess. X X X.*

Evening wasn't a good time to be in the Capri. You could catch things off the tables then that you'd normally only catch from toilet seats. You never knew who or what might sit next to you.

I was tired. I wanted to feel the softness of my own bed. I wanted my slippers, the evening paper and a mug of Horlicks. Instead, I slouched along the street and pushed open the door of the café. Tess was sat at the same table as on that previous occasion. She was even sat at the same seat. Two yobs played pool noisily up by the counter, and a vagrant was asleep at the table near the fruit machine.

'What is it, Tess?' I said, trying to get straight to the point. She was inappropriately dressed for the Capri at this time of the evening. Her cream silk shirt was tied in a knot to fasten it about the waist, and as usual, she wasn't wearing anything beneath it. It's advisable to wear a bra in the Capri: some of the men there do, too. The silk was fairly sheer and, on a clear day, you could probably see the coast of France. I could certainly see her tits as plain as the nose on her face. With it she wore a tight mini-skirt with a multi-coloured pattern, that looked as though Salvador Dali had designed it during a nightmare. Her high-heeled cream shoes made her calves look muscular. The yobs at the back of the café were casting lustful glances in Tess's direction, which is probably what she was craving.

'After you left this afternoon, I got dressed and went across to see Eddie English,' she announced.

'I hope he appreciated the outfit,' I said.

'He wasn't there. When I drove back home, I saw two men coming out of my house. I was scared, Jack, so I didn't stop. I just put my foot down and headed here.'

'Did they follow you?' I asked.

'I don't think so.'

'What did they look like?'

'There was a big man, well over six feet tall and a shorter man, ugly with turn-ups on his jeans. They definitely weren't there to read the gas meter.'

'They're the same blokes who doused me in petrol. They

96

work for English. Why did you go to see him, by the way?' I asked.

'I wanted him to try and persuade Paul to put his faith in British justice and plead Not Guilty to Michelle's murder. English carries more weight than me. I'm just Paul's wife.'

Cheesy Vic came across, holding a pool cue he'd been putting a new tip on.

'Can I get you folks anything, or are you just using this dump as a meeting place?' A fag hung precariously from the corner of his mouth.

'We'll have two cappuccinos, Vic,' I said, knowing he only served cheap instant stuff. He wandered off.

One yob, wearing a royal blue shell suit and with his baseball cap on back to front, got brave and shouted, 'Hey, darling, get yer tits oot for the lads.'

I grabbed the cue Vic was holding and walked with it to the pool table. 'Do you want to ask the lady a proper question?' I said.

The yob laughed. 'Fuck you.'

I held the cue aloft and brought it crashing down on his head. The cue snapped in two and the yob fell to the café's dirty floor. His mate decided against involvement.

'Tell your pal when he comes round that I played a foul stroke and he's entitled to two free shots.' Vic held the broken cue pieces and had obviously thought ahead to repairing it.

I went back to Tess and said, 'Come on, I'll drive you home.'

She made sure her car was locked up for the night and then got into my Golf in as ladylike a fashion as possible in such a tight skirt. The sky had turned ominously the colour of a wet hippo's arse and we'd barely found a gap in the traffic before the first rumble of thunder could be heard. Splashes of rain hit the windscreen and drivers began switching on headlamps. It was storm time, and the rain came down in those torrents that bounce off the pavements and wet you twice, once on the way down and again on the way up. People dressed in summerwear ran into doorways and bus shelters to seek refuge. I had the screen wipers on full throttle to give me some visibility.

The weather got worse on the northern side of the city, as if we were driving into the very eye of the storm. Rainwater swept down the roads like a dam had burst, and the spray from the vehicle in front made things even more difficult. The nutters were out in force, driving nose to tail at sixty miles an hour, so I gave them a wide berth. As we negotiated the traffic island on Chester Road at Thornhill Road, Streetly, I became aware of two headlights on full beam behind. The lights were bright enough to make it painful to look in the rearview mirror. Whoever it was, was driving about three yards behind us at fifty miles an hour. I slowed to let him overtake. He slowed, too.

I think that's when I got that sinking feeling in the pit of my stomach. I slowed right down to twenty miles an hour and the car behind deliberately bumped us. Tess became aware of what was happening through the whiplash effect we felt.

'What's he doing?' she said in alarm, turning to look behind us.

'I think we've got company,' I muttered, accelerating away in second gear, up the incline towards the lights at Bridle Lane. I changed into third and began to ask questions of the VW's 1300 engine that nobody had a right to ask. The car behind stayed with us all the way. The lights were on red and two cars were ahead of us at the lights.

'Hold tight,' I said, overtaking the stationary vehicles and shooting through the junction. There was a cacophony of tooting horns left in our wake. The pursuing vehicle was still no more than ten yards behind and we were doing seventy plus. Visibility was abysmal as I could just make out the green lights at the Foley Road junction. Some turd began reversing from a drive on our left and I had to swerve to avoid him and then swerve back to avoid the single decker bus coming towards us. Tess had her hands to her face in total disbelief. This felt like the ideal time to foul my trousers. Hardwick Road lights were green as we aquaplaned through at eighty miles an hour and hit the long stretch of straight road before the Chester Road begins twisting and turning more times than a Conservative government.

At that point, our back windscreen shattered and showered us with glass.

'What was that?' Tess screamed.

'Probably a bullet,' I said, trying to sound casual. 'I think they're trying to attract our attention.' I wondered where the bullet might have ended up. We passed the Old Irish Harp at ninety and then I nearly lost it on the left-hand bend. I knew there was a big dip in the road which encourages flooding whenever there's heavy rain about a mile further on, so I had to slow right down to sixty and move over into the other carriageway, causing some guy in a Transit van to slam on his brakes and mount the kerb. 'That was fucking close,' I shouted. The adrenalin was pumping. I could feel it trickling down my leg. This guy was proving harder to shake off than a summer cold.

'What are we going to do, Jack?' Tess asked. I was too busy trying to keep the car on the road to answer her. I had just spotted a prat in a Metro doing fifteen miles an hour, seconds before we hit him, and took avoiding action by overtaking him on the inside. Maybe they call that 'under-taking'. I daresay it scared the guy at the wheel shitless. We were approaching the lights at Shire Oak now, and I knew it wasn't a good idea to run a red light there as the chances were you'd collide with a truck the size of a Saturn V and end up spoiling some traffic cop's night as the poor sod filled in all the stats forms.

The lights were amber. I took a chance: it paid off. I heard the car horns as our pursuers did likewise. They were still behind us. The pedestrian lights at Anchor Bridge were turning red as we approached, and I could see two soaked figures on the left kerb about to step into the road. I kept my hand on the car horn and maintained speed. The pedestrians jumped back onto the footpath and got splashed for their trouble. I knew Brownhills High Street would slow us down to walking pace, so I changed down to third and skidded left into Silver Street and used it as a by-pass.

I stayed in third until the real tight bend which takes the road back towards the High Street, when I dropped into second and our speed slowed below twenty. Then I accelerated up the hill and shot across the roundabout. Two cars slammed on the anchors to avoid me and hit each other.

I screeched right into The Parade, and then kicked myself for not thinking of pulling into Brownhills Police Station. It would probably have been closed, anyway. The car behind was still with us and we were closing in on home territory. Unfortunately, I had no ideas to put to Tess about escaping the predicament unscathed.

The lights at the A5 junction shone green. In White Horse Road I managed, with consummate ease, to bounce off a few parked cars as the Golf got driven offcourse by the many pot-holes in the street. It is said that the holes in the tarmac in White Horse Road can be followed through to the limestone caverns of the Peak District. I knew there was a hump-back bridge ahead; the road twisted right and then sharp left as you crossed the narrow bridge. I'd have to slow down from seventy.

'Better get ready to make a run for it, Tess. We ain't gonna shake these guys off,' I warned.

'I can't run in this skirt,' she said. I was half-expecting her to ask for a moment to touch-up her make-up.

'Take the bloody thing off, then,' I snarled, 'unless you want to stay with the car and negotiate a surrender. I promise to identify your body in the mortuary.'

I heard her unzip the frankly *tacky* skirt and my peripheral vision enjoyed the sight of her easing it over her thighs and down into the footwell. She kicked off the heeled shoes as well. I swear she folded the skirt neatly before releasing her seat belt.

I hit the brakes, shifted into third and skidded across the bridge, praying nothing was coming the other way. We scraped along the wall on the nearside before regaining momentum and gathering velocity in Wharf Lane. I decided we'd make a run for it across the wasteland between Chasetown and Chasewater, or the Chasewater North Shore Parkland as it was properly titled. It didn't matter what it was called, since it would soon have the Burntwood By-pass ploughing through it.

I nearly blew up the engine by taking the Highfields Road hill at sixty in third gear before slewing into peaceful Church Street.

'This street's a dead-end, Tess. Get ready to run. Stay close, okay?' She didn't answer. She was as scared as I was. I put my foot to the floor and passed St Anne's Church at a cool fifty-five, then stamped on the brakes as we got to Chasetown FC's ground and brought the car skidding to a halt in the gravelled area at the end of the road.

'Now!' I shouted. 'Run that way,' pointing right. Tess leapt out into the torrential rain as I put the car into reverse and slammed it into our pursuers' car.

I jumped out and ran after Tess, hoping I'd slowed them down sufficiently with the impact to give us a decent head-start. Tess was twenty yards ahead of me, running bare-footed and now wearing just her flimsy silk blouse and pink, fluted briefs cut high on the legs. Both garments were already soaked-through and clinging to her skin. I became aware of my injured knee and knew I wasn't in shape for long-distance running. My shoes let in the rainwater and my strides were already about five times heavier than when I put them on. Looking behind, I could see two fellahs getting out of the crashed grey saloon. When they took up the chase I knew we were in trouble.

Even with my damaged knee I soon caught up with Tess as we ran across a grassy area near the rugby club changing rooms. There was a metal barrier we had to hurdle. I was getting severe jogger's nipple and I imagined Tess was, too. I kind of hoped we'd get through this and I could give them some attention . . . There was a fence ahead – well, part fence, part boundary hedge. We got through into a flat area used for tipping. Looked like somebody had been emptying their skips there. I nearly lost my balance after treading on half a house-brick.

'Keep going, Tess,' I shouted, my mouth filling with rain.

We took a muddy path to our left between heaps of rubble. A flash of lightning lit up the sky and I could see the electricity pylons in the distance. I heard the two guys chasing us shout something. No doubt it wasn't complimentary.

It was like a cross-country run. Every second step ended with your foot in a six-inch-deep puddle. I pitied Tess, having to run barefoot. Her jogging outfit was something to behold, though. A couple of times I thought I heard gunshots, but your mind tends to play tricks when you're being chased by two madmen in a thunderstorm. By now I knew the two weren't the guys who beat me up. No way could the big man have run this far. I also knew they weren't chasing us to sell pension plans. Even time-share salesmen didn't go this far.

Eventually, the dumped car tyres, corrugated sheeting and old tea chests gave way to the old mine area. I'd been here before in daylight; it looks like a lunar landscape, the ground covered in the dark blue-grey nutty slack from the old mine workings. This was the area of the Number Four pit, opened in the mid-nineteenth century. Ten pits were sunk in the vicinity, and all had closed by the time Spurs did the double in 1961. I kept my eyes peeled in the vain hope of finding a secret IRA arms cache. Even a carelessly discarded pick-axe would have done. Like coppers, there's never one around when you want one.

I knew we were both close to exhaustion and we'd have to try and hide. A boggy dip in the ground full of bulrushes slowed us down. The black and yellow triangular sign on the barbed wire fence ahead stated: DANGER. DEEP WATER AND SLURRY. We headed right for the grass-covered slag heaps, criss-crossed with muddy paths, and the haunt of weekend motorbike scramblers. I spotted a hollow, covered in dense undergrowth, as we got to the top of the mound, and grabbed Tess by the blouse, pulling her down to the ground, where we found ourselves in six inches of mud.

'Cover yourself in mud – it'll act as camouflage.' I began hurriedly slapping mud on my face, hands, and anywhere else I could reach. Tess did the same. I smeared her back and legs and we lay face down in the stuff, hardly daring to move or breathe. It seemed like a week of Sundays before anything happened. Tess's hair was now mud-streaked and matted to her muddy face. The heavy rain had turned more to drizzle and I watched Tess's body rise and fall with each heavy breath she took.

Looking up I saw two feet, about eighteen inches from my face: two Nike cross-trainers, about size nine. The heels faced towards me, so whoever occupied them was looking in the opposite direction. Either that, or he was a freak. I decided to grab his legs and pull him down. I lunged at both ankles and tugged with all the strength left in me. With the help of the slippery ground, the body of a white male bodybuilder, with long hair like some Californian rock star, crashed face downwards. He was holding a handgun. I smashed my right fist into his left temple, twice, and the brute parted with his senses long enough for me to grab the gun and pistol-whip him into deep sleep.

The gun was a .45 calibre automatic. I thought it might come in useful so I held onto it. I also made a point of not tucking it into my waistband like they do in the movies, for fear of shooting my dick off.

Crouching, I moved off down the slope of the mound towards the fenced-off pools. A black bodybuilder stood with his back to the fence. It was Errol, the man with the Ratner's-smile, holding a baseball bat in his right mitt. He finally spotted me approaching him, but he clearly didn't notice the gun.

'Time to die, Mayo,' he said, raising the bat in what I have to report was a threatening manner.

'I see your bat, Errol, and raise you one fucking gun,' I said, aiming the weapon somewhere between his lungs and his intestines. The look on his face was one of disbelief marinated in a sauce of fear. He still came towards me. I pulled the trigger.

Click. Nothing happened. I tried again. *Click*. Still nothing. I threw the gun at the guy and it bounced off his chest like a tennis ball. I raced at Errol and gathered enough momentum to take us both crashing through the wire fence and into the slurry. The cold dark water engulfed us both. The difference was, I could swim. Errol panicked and began thrashing about.

'I can't swim,' he squealed before his mouth refilled with water.

'So I gather,' I replied, climbing back onto the side. There's never a lifeguard around either, when you need one. Errol really needed one. Soon he was floating face down in the water like a nocturnal snorkeller.

I tossed the gun into the water and went to get Tess.

'What happened?' she shivered.

'Errol's a goner,' I replied, 'and we better make ourselves scarce before the other bozo wakes up.'

'Did you kill him, Jack?'

'No. Come on, let's go.' I took her arm and led her off towards Cannock Road. The rain had stopped altogether, now. The other guy was still pushing out the zeds and looked like he'd be non *compos mentis* until around mid-July.

It took another twenty minutes to get through the increasingly dense undergrowth. We trudged through mud and grit, and under low branches, swearing at the sharp twigs before finally emerging where Burntwood Road meets the A5190 Cannock Road. I knew Cannock was to the west because a sign told me, proudly, that Cannock was a 'nuclear free zone', whatever the hell that meant. We headed east, towards Chase Terrace.

'Well, Jack, now what?' Tess asked, trying to cover her upper body with the ripped remains of a once-stylish silk blouse.

'We can't go to your place 'cos it's being watched. And I can't take a near-naked girl to my place because my wife would instigate divorce proceedings. I'll call Ralph and we'll go back to the office.' I looked at the mud-smeared dial of my watch and it read eleven-fifteen. It was eleven-thirty when I stood in the telephone kiosk at Burntwood Shopping Centre looking for money to call Ralph. I found two sodden fivers and a twenty-pence coin. I dialled the office after depositing the coin and waited for my partner to answer. Eventually a voice croaked down the line.

'You better have a fuckin' good reason for calling at this time whoever you are,' Ralph growled.

'Ralph, it's Jack,' I said.

'Jack?'

'Your partner. Shut up and listen. Tess and I are at the Burntwood Shopping Centre. We're in trouble and need you here. You got that?'

'Yeah. What sort of trouble?' Ralph asked.

'I'll explain when you get here.'

'I'm on my way. Give me twenty minutes.'

'Oh, and Ralph—'

'Yeah?'

'Remind me to have a word with you some time about your telephone manner.' I hung up the receiver.

Tess and I stood in the doorway of the Bill Stickers' pub and waited for Ralph. It was nearly thirty minutes later when Ralph's blue Allegro screeched to a halt. We got inside the car and Ralph swung it round towards Lichfield.

'Where to, Jack?' he asked.

'The office, Ralph. We need to consider our next move.' Ralph stank of booze and appeared to have trouble staying awake, which can be disconcerting at sixty miles an hour.

'How did you get on with Maggie?' I asked.

'I left just after you did. What's this trouble you're in? And why do you both look like mud-wrestlers?'

'When I got back to our office, Tess was there. She'd found her house being watched. I drove her back to take a look and a car started to follow us. Noticeably.'

'How do you mean?' Ralph asked, picking his nose.

'They fired a shot at us, smashing my rear screen.'

'Gunshot?'

'Nah – catapult. Yes, *a gunshot*, Ralph. We tried to shake 'em off but couldn't so I drove to the wasteland by Chasewater and we made a run for it.'

'Who were they?'

'Two bodybuilders. One was Errol, the black guy from the Amazon Gym with a smile like a prospector's dream. The other was white with long hair. I clubbed the white guy to the ground and gave Errol precise directions to the bottom of a pool of slurry. He is, at this moment, soaking overnight like a dried apricot.'

'He's dead, Jack? Are you saying you killed a bloke?'

Ralph was smirking. I nodded. 'Stone me! That was always my ambition, you know, to kill somebody in the line of duty. Preferably a crook or a senior officer – and not necessarily in that order.' Ralph perked up. I'd really gone up in his estimation.

You think you know the bloke you're working with – and then you discover that the peak of his professional ambition is to snuff somebody out. I believed him. I believed anything Ralph told me. And I believed *everything* I heard about him. For instance, he once drank a pint of his own urine as a bet. He 'borrowed' a police Land Rover and towed a gypsy's caravan from where it had been parked on wasteground on his beat and left it on a traffic island out in Worcestershire. He used to arrest drunks and instead of charging them, would cut down on paperwork by just dumping them miles out in the countryside. Then he'd take their shoes and discard them elsewhere. He got away with murder. Probably.

It was after midnight when Ralph knocked over the No Waiting sign and brought us to a halt in front of the office. There was some sort of trouble outside Srinegar Mo's place, with white-shirted Asian waiters in the middle of some pushing and shoving with a couple of pissed Brums. Ralph walked over.

'They didn't pay their bills, Ralph,' explained the emaciated waiter with the Zapata moustache.

'Fuck off, you Paki bastards,' the Brum with bleached blond hair said, in a broad accent.

Ralph picked him up by his neck and groin and threw him through the glass window of the WMT bus shelter, where he failed to beat the count. His mate was already fumbling with some cash to settle the bill.

'Don't forget the tip, pal,' Ralph reminded him politely. The youth scarpered, leaving the mouthy one in a pile of glass crystals and blood.

The Asian waiters looked across at the state Tess and I were in, and obviously decided against inviting us inside. We stepped past Claude, who had brought something up over the steps, and went inside. Upstairs, Ralph put the kettle on while Tess took first use of the shower. Ralph and I looked out the window and watched the bus-shelter yob pick himself up and limp off home.

'Jack, we're not getting anywhere on this case, are we?' Ralph asked, still looking out the window.

'What do you suggest?' I countered.

'We've been doing everything like cops. Dotting the Is and crossing the Ts like we were still governed by the soddin' Police and Criminal Evidence Act and all the other crap that used to tie our hands. Now we're *private* detectives we can do what the hell we like. We can't lose our jobs 'cos we already lost them. Now we're our own business.'

'I might regret asking this, Ralph, but what are you getting at?'

'We know Paul didn't kill Michelle, else we wouldn't be doing this. We're pretty sure Barry Raphael was involved in the murder somewhere along the line.'

'Go on,' I said.

'If we take English out of the game we can get Paul represented by Jacobs, for a start. We can question English without worrying about his rights and we can put pressure on Raphael. If they're involved in the death, we might start getting to the bottom of it.'

'And if they're not?'

'You've got a better idea?' he asked.

I poured three mugs of coffee and took a sip from mine. I looked at Ralph who was waiting for an answer and getting impatient.

'You killed a guy tonight, Jack. At the worst you could have the kidnapping of English taken into consideration.'

'Okay, Ralph. Let's do it,' I said, and the hideous thought of sharing a slop-out bucket with my partner flashed through my mind.

CHAPTER 8

I was already having misgivings about Ralph's plan when Tess came back into the office, wet from her shower and wrapped in something Ralph used as a towel, duster and dish-cloth. She was just about decent.

'I used your shampoo, Ralph. I hope you don't mind,' she said, bunching her wet hair in her hands and holding it away from her face. 'Have you got an old shirt or something I could wear?'

'Me, too, Ralph,' I said, heading for the shower. 'Nothing Romanian, though.' Ralph was having inter-crural thoughts of Tess but managed a slight nod.

I quickly cleaned up and put on the clothes he had brought in for me – a red polo shirt, jeans, socks and a pair of rather malodorous training shoes with holes in the sole of each.

We went down to the car. Tess, wearing Ralph's un-washed striped pyjama jacket, insisted on coming with us. There was no changing Ralph's mind, now. He'd got the green light and his tunnel vision took over. You'd more likely get a round of applause from the Venus de Milo than get Ralph to hang back.

It was the middle of the night when we got into Lichfield, and the place was deserted. At this time of night in Birmingham, the last of the stragglers from the clubs would be off in search of a greasy kebab or somewhere private they could take a leak, like up against the front door of Digbeth Police Station or from the footbridge over Suffolk Street.

Ralph quickly went through his plan, such as it was.

'We set off the alarm at English's office. The local cops arrive and the keyholder is turfed out of bed. Hopefully, that's our Eddie. The cops are satisfied that nothing much is afoot and return to the nick for a well-earned cup of char. Eddie stays behind to reset the alarm. We move in and snaffle the dummy.'

It sounded feasible. I suppose the Yanks' plan for rescuing the hostages from Tehran sounded feasible – and what a bag of rats that turned into.

Ralph parked up in the pay and display car park adjacent to Minster Pool. Tess reluctantly agreed to stay with the car when we nominated her as getaway driver and left her the keys. Ralph and I walked to Erasmus Darwin Chambers and down the side entry. There was a gate to the back yard which we climbed over, only to find it was unlocked. We made our way up the black metal fire escape until we reached the first floor and the rear of Eddie English's offices. When Ralph put the window in, the sound of breaking glass must have been heard in Rugeley.

'That's a soft touch you've got there, Ralph,' I complimented him as we hurried to find somewhere to hide to watch the ensuing events. We split up. Ralph blended into the darkness of Friar's Alley, while I hid near the Arts Centre. Within minutes a Maestro decked out in the livery of Staffordshire Police and bearing the famous Staffordshire knot as emblems on the doors, pulled up. A regular cop got out of the driving seat and a special constable climbed out of the passenger side. They mumbled news of their arrival to their controller via personal radio. The special remained at the front of the building while the regular went round the back. It all went quiet for twenty minutes or so until a familiar BMW saloon pulled up behind the Maestro. Eddie English got out wearing one of those leisure suits that the older generation insist on wearing. The colour, pink, did little for his machismo. He opened the front door and entered.

I waited maybe five minutes before the two cops came out and bade good night to English, then drove off towards Beacon Street. Eddie, as I'd hoped, was slack enough to leave the door unlocked. Ralph got there before me and we ran up the stairs, reaching Eddie's office before he'd even opened the door.

'What on earth do you think you're doing! Leave at once or I shall call the police.' The guy wasn't pleased to see us. He was even less pleased when Ralph poked him in his right eye with his chubby index finger. He sat down on one of those ugly leather and chrome chairs and held his face.

'Where's the paperwork on the Johnson case, shithead?' Ralph has a healthy disrespect for solicitors, feeling they share the same rung on the great social ladder of life as child molesters and tinker tarmac gangs.

'I really can't see what you hope to achieve,' English said, just seconds before Ralph pulled him up from the seat by his ear and thrust his hand down the front of the brief's briefs. The look on English's face told me what Ralph was gripping and his comments to Eddie confirmed it.

'Either you answer our questions or I'm gonna turn you into a fuckin' eunuch. Now, *where's the paperwork?*' Ralph looked like he meant what he said.

'It's all on my desk,' English gasped. 'Everything's there.'

I went into Eddie's sumptuous office and gathered up all the documentation, putting it into a box-file I'd emptied on the floor.

'Got it, Ralph,' I said. 'Let's go.'

Ralph jerked English to his feet and pulled him towards the door.

'Where are we going? Where are you taking me?' English yelped.

'Your final resting place, you bent bastard,' Ralph said in a less than complimentary fashion. 'Did you get the headed paper, Jack?'

'Yeah. Let's go.'

Ralph marched Eddie outside while I switched off the lights and locked up. We returned to the car park and I left Eddie's office keys in the middle of Minster Pool, where they'd be handy for him. Tess started up the car. I sat alongside her while Ralph bundled Eddie into the rear.

'What did you mean by "final resting place", Mr Grice?' he finally plucked up the courage to ask.

'Let me put it this way, Ed. Your clients will have to contact you using a ouija board. Get my drift?' Ralph was enjoying himself. Terror and intimidation came naturally to him.

'Back to the office, Tess,' I said, admiring the sweep of her thighs on the torn PVC driver's seat.

We made good time and arrived back just as the Asian milk trucks began taking to the streets. Ralph shoved Eddie into the bedsit and bound him with speaker wire before handcuffing him to the bed. As a final threat, he took off his right sock and stuffed it into English's mouth. I felt that was contrary to the spirit of the Geneva Convention but I let it ride.

Back in the office, Tess was bending over the tray making coffee. The jacket had ridden up her back somewhat, exposing her bare buttocks. Ralph studied her, then gave me the sort of look which indicated he'd sell his own mother to the Arabs for a night with Tess. Quite why the Arabs would want to buy Ralph's mother, who is just a smaller, though hairer, version of him I really wouldn't know.

'Don't stand like that, Tess,' he said, 'you're inviting crime.' Tess giggled and handed us both a mug of coffee. We each took some of the paperwork and began to sift through it.

'I've got the statement here from the doctor who pronounced death,' I said.

'Read it out loud, Jack,' Ralph replied, sitting with his feet on his desk.

I began reading from the witness statement. 'Statement of Dr John Rivera, over 21 years, occupation: registrar. "I was on duty in the casualty department of the Good Hope Hospital, Sutton Coldfield on Wednesday 7 June 1992 at 04.15 hours . . ." ' I broke off and looked at Tess, who was sitting crosslegged on the floor.

'Didn't you tell me that Michelle was found in the early hours of *Tuesday* morning?' I asked, trying to clear up an ambiguity.

'Possibly. I was confused, Jack. It's not every day you find your husband in prison on a murder charge.' I went back to reading out loud.

' ". . . when a young female of approximately 23 years was admitted as an emergency. The only history available was that she had sustained a stab injury to the left side of her chest." That's very interesting,' I said.

'So she was still alive when she got to the hospital. She *wasn't* found dead at the scene.' Ralph was thinking along the same lines as me. 'I wonder if we've got statements from the two kids who found the body?'

'We'll have to look in a minute.' I carried on. ' "On admission she had a clear airway and was breathing spontaneously, but this was sporadic. There was no cardiac output and her pupils were fixed and dilated with no response to light. There was a puncture wound one a half centimetres in length in the left fifth intercostal space, four centimetres from the midline. Immediate resuscitation was commenced with intubation and ventilation. Intravenous access was gained and pericardiocentesis revealed fresh blood. Thoracotomy was performed as an emergency, and a puncture wound through the lung and into the left ventricle of the heart was identified. The pericardial sac was full of clotted blood. She was bleeding profusely from the wound in the heart and this was sutured. Though this effectively arrested the bleeding, the heart stopped shortly afterwards and despite aggressive attempts at resuscitation it was impossible to regain cardiac activity. Resuscitation was abandoned at 05.15 hours on 7 June 1992 at which time the patient was declared deceased. Signed, J. Rivera." '

I put the statement face down on the desk.

Ralph piped up, after releasing some trapped gas through a belch loud enough to wake the dead. 'I've got the pathologist's report here. "Statement of Dr A. P. Pozniak, age over 21, occupation: pathologist. Report on the autopsy of the body of Michelle Susan ROSA, aged 24 years, made at the mortuary, Stafford at 10 a.m. on Wednesday 7 June 1992, acting on the instructions of HM Coroner for South Staffordshire District by virtue of Section 19 Coroner's Act 1988. Date and time of death – 7 June 1992 at 05.15 hours. Place of death – Good Hope Hospital, Sutton Coldfield. Other doctors present at autopsy– Dr Khalique. Circumstances: I have been informed by Detective Superintendent Smith, CID, of Staffordshire Police, that Miss Rosa was involved in an incident on wasteground near Chasewater, Staffordshire. She received an injury and, on arrival at Good Hope Hospital, she was gravely ill. From the hospital casualty notes and from information supplied to me by Dr Khalique, I have learned that Miss Rosa had a single penetrating wound of the left side of the chest. There was no cardiac output. Vigorous resuscitation was undertaken and a left thoracotomy was performed. This disclosed a haemopericardium due to laceration of the left ventricle. The wound was sutured but although a transient heartbeat was obtained, the patient died at 05.15. Post mortem examination: present . . ." He gives a list of the people at the post mortem,' Ralph interjected, 'everyone up to and including Uncle Tom Cobbleigh. One, two, three detectives, the Coroner's Officer, Scenes of Crime Officer (SOCO), photographer, Identifying Officer and a mortuary technician who probably munched on a sausage and egg sandwich throughout.

'Get on with it, Ralph,' I said.

He continued to read. ' "The body was that of a young Caucasian woman of slim but athletic build. Noted height 5'6". Weight 54.48 kg (8st 8lbs). There were no remarkable natural external features. A tiny incised wound of the right upper chest was confirmed as therapeutic. The cervical and upper chest procedures had produced considerable haemorrhage into soft tissues. An extensive left thoracotomy incision incorporated an incised wound of the chest and is described fully below. All needles, cannulae, tubes and tapes had been removed from the body before arrival at the mortuary. External signs of injury: one. A penetrating wound of the left side of the chest, in the fifth left intercostal space, close to the sternal border had been incorporated in a 165mm thoracotomy incision and its presence can only be determined by reference to the hospital casualty notes, confirmed to me by Dr Khalique, and by the position of underlying wounds to which it must have been related. It is described in the notes as being 1½ cm long (15mm) which is in keeping with the size of the deeper wounds and also with the dimensions in cuts in a blouse worn by the deceased (see below). Two. A sutured slit 10 mm long was present at the lateral extremity of the left side of the upper lip. This injury could have been caused during therapeutic intubation as it is not recorded in the hospital notes. Dr Khalique had no first-hand knowledge of this wound. Three. Two very small bruises were present on the outer aspect of the left chest, a little way about the costal margin. Internal injuries: these were confined to the left side of the chest.

' "Owing to surgery, the traverse of the chest wall by the wounding weapon could not be determined. The pericardium had been widely opened surgically but it was heavily infiltrated by blood through the whole of its preserved part. There was a sutured incised wound of the anterior wall of the left ventricle of the heart, close to the septum. On removing the sutures it could be demonstrated that the wound extended through the wall of the ventricle, but that the posterior wall of the heart was not injured. This wound measured 15 mm. A 5-mm incised wound, also penetrating the left ventricular wall, was present just medial to the main wound and a 4 mm penetrating wound was found 15 mm lateral to and a little above the major wound. Neither of these injuries had been sutured.

' "In its passage across the pleural space, the wounding weapon had just nicked the medial border of the upper lobe of the left lung. A massive left haemothorax had resulted from these injuries.

' "Internal examination . . ." I won't read out all the bloody weights,' Ralph said, before pressing on.

' "Central nervous system: skull, meninges, brain and cerebral arteries normal. There was just the slightest 'stickiness' of the brain on slicing, to suggest that brain death may have occurred before surgery could be undertaken. Respiratory system: upper respiratory tract normal. Pleurae healthy (apart from injury on left side). The lungs were healthy apart from basal and posterior collapse consistent with artificial ventilation.

' "Cardiovascular system: apart from the injury to the heart, its valves and coronary arteries were normal, as were the aorta and the great vessels. Gastro-intestinal system: oesophagus, stomach, small and large bowels, normal. Liver normal. Gall bladder and pancreas normal. The stomach contained only fluid with a few bits of vegetable. Urogenital system: kidneys normal. No shock effect. Bladder full of slightly cloudy urine. Genitalia uninjured. Evidence of recent sexual activity. Reticuloendothelial system: spleen normal. No lymphadenopathy. Endocrine system: thyroid, adrenals, pituitary gland normal. Cause of death: one, haemorrhage; two, penetrating wound of the heart. Comment: Miss Rosa was a very healthy young woman. A single wound has penetrated the heart causing rapidly fatal haemorrhage. The presence of two subsidiary punctures in the heart does not indicate more than one penetration . . ." '

The use of the word 'penetration' set Ralph's mind wandering and his eyes drifted from the statement to the gaping hole in Tess's pyjama top.

'Go on, Ralph,' I said impatiently, and he lit up one of his cheap, slim cigars and went back to his reading. A smell not dissimilar to mature yak shit filled the office.

' ". . . penetration," ' he continued, ' "by the wounding weapon, but probably indicates that the weapon was not withdrawn in a single movement. Partial withdrawal could result in these further wounds occurring from the contract-ing and expanding nature of the heart's movements. No defence wounds were found. Measurement of the heart wound and of cuts present in a blouse worn by Miss Rosa and produced for my inspection by Mr Metcalf, SOCO, which all measured 15 mm in length, indicate a quite narrow-bladed weapon (little more than 2 cm in blade diameter). The depth of penetration, to reach only the anterior wall of the heart suggests a small blade, perhaps only 10 cm long or even shorter. As the indications are of a small weapon, it probably penetrated to the hilt. It would have required only moderate force for a sharp blade to have achieved this degree of penetration. Addendum: surgery and medical treatment, although failing to save life, were not factors in the cause of death. Signed, et cetera, et cetera." John Wayne would have called it a "flesh wound", Jack,' Ralph added, drawing on his vast ignorance. He blew his nose, loudly, into something resembling Diane from next door's undergarments.

'I've got the statement from the Scenes of Crime Officer, Jack,' Tess said, lying back and leaning on her right elbow.

'Let's hear it, then.'

' "Derek Metcalf. Over 21. Scenes of Crime Officer in Staffordshire Police, based at Lichfield Police Station. At 04.40 hours on Wednesday 7 June 1992 I attended an area on the north shore of Chasewater, near Chasetown in Staffordshire. This was the scene of an earlier incident during which a young woman received injuries from which she later died. Parked amidst the bushes, some five metres from the water's edge was a red Citroën AX car, registration blah, blah, blah, which was seen to be heavily bloodstained in the area of the driver's seat. I took a sample and control sample of the blood from the driver's seat which I refer to as DM/1. From the rear of the same car I recovered a green T-shirt, size large. This shirt had been draped over the centre of the rear seat. I found no evidence of blood on this shirt, which I produce as ref. DM/2. At 10.00 a.m. on Wednesday 7 June 1992 I attended the post mortem examination of Michelle Rosa, deceased, at Stafford Mortuary. During the course of this examination I was handed the following items recovered from the deceased by the pathologist, Dr Pozniak. Blood, reference APP/1, blood for alcohol analysis ref. APP/2, urine, ref. APP/3 and urine for alcohol analysis, ref. APP/4. These items were all packaged and sealed and signed by Dr Pozniak. During the course of the post mortem, some items of clothing belonging to the deceased were brought into the mortuary, from which I took possession of the following items: bloodstained white blouse, reference DM/3, bloodstained denim shorts, ref.

DM/4 and bloodstained white panties, reference DM/5. I was handed the following further items by Dr Pozniak from the body of the deceased: vaginal swabs, references APP/5 and APP/6, cut and combed pubic hair samples, references APP/7 and APP/8.

' "I removed all these items to Lichfield Police Station. I placed items APP/1 and APP/3 in the deep freezer in the scenes of crime store. I placed items APP/2 and APP/4 in the refrigerator in the doctor's room in the cell block at Lichfield Police Station. Items DM/3, DM/4 and DM/5 were heavily bloodstained and hung up to air-dry in the forensic store. Items marked APP/5 and APP/6 were stored in the aforementioned refrigerator.

' "At 12.00 p.m. that same day I attended the blood bank, Haemotology Department, Good Hope Hospital, where I was handed a sealed specimen of blood, reference number 34735, by Mr Eric Thomas. I produce this as exhibit ref. DM/6. At 4.15 p.m. the same day I attended the male locker room at the Amazon Gym, Lichfield, where I was met by Detective Constable Buchan of Lichfield CID. From a metal locker bearing the name Paul Johnson, DC Buchan showed me a small folding knife with a brass-bound wooden handle. The knife was in a closed position, with the blade hidden from view. The knife was photographed *in situ* by the Force photographer; Mr McCreadie and I then recovered it and caused it to be sealed and labelled as reference DM/7.

' "DC Buchan also showed me a pair of pink ladies' panties from the same locker which were also photographed and recovered by me as reference DM/8. I conveyed the knife immediately to the Fingerprint Bureau at Staffordshire Police HQ where I handed it to Detective Sergeant Leggatt.

' "At 11.00 a.m. on Thursday 8 June 1992, I was present at Lichfield Police Station. Police surgeon Dr Ahmed Veshwani handed me the following items from the prisoner Paul Johnson: cut and combed pubic hair, refs AV/1 and

AV/2, penile swabs, references AV/3 and AV/4, and blood samples, refs AV/5, AV/6 and AV/7.

' "At 14.35 p.m. that same day I attended the Forensic Science Laboratory in Birmingham and handed over the following items to Forensic Scientist Sarah Hearn: references DM/1, DM/2, APP/1, APP/2, et cetera et cetera . . ." All very neat, eh Jack?' Tess tossed down the statement and flicked back her hair.

Ralph took a last drag of his rancid cigar before dropping it into the remains of his coffee.

'Several things spring to my mind,' I said, trying to come across as if I knew what I was talking about. 'Michelle was still alive when the two boys got to her. I haven't seen their statements yet. Also, we assumed the panties found in Paul's locker were the ones she was wearing at the time of her death – unless she was wearing two pairs, which is highly unlikely. And, as only moderate force was needed to stab Michelle, maybe her killer wasn't a man.'

'Maybe we should take this opportunity to question Silly Bollocks next door,' said Ralph, cracking his knuckles.

'I agree. Then we'd better consider moving him from here. This would be one of the first places Raphael would look. Got any suggestions, Ralph?' It was a stupid question.

'How about the canals at Fradley Junction? Tied securely to something heavy, like a paving slab.'

'I thought we might keep him alive, if that's okay with you.' I looked at Ralph.

'I'll drag him to my brother's place in Nechells. The locals are used to hearing screams. Tony can put him up for a few days.'

'Let's go see him, then.'

English looked a sorry sight, cuffed to the foot of Ralph's bed and nearly choking on my colleague's sweaty sock. He was visibly moved when I recovered the oral obstruction.

'I'll see you both pay for this,' he said, by way of thanks.

'We're here to ask you some questions,' I said.

'I wouldn't give you the steam off my piss,' he answered.

'That's hardly the language of the gentleman Ralph and I have come to know and love. I must tell you, of course, that you don't have to say anything. You have the right to remain silent. Permanently. Get my drift?' I'd crouched down to get a better view of the expressions on English's face. Ralph appeared to be kneeling on his reproductive organs to get his avid attention.

'You're wasting your breath, Mayo,' English said, just a split second before Ralph slapped him hard across the face.

'I want you to know, fuckpig, that I like to do things by the book. Unfortunately for you, it's a book by the Marquis de Sade,' grinned Ralph, as he whacked English again with the back of his hand.

'Why did you send those two goons to my office to work me over?' I asked.

'Look, Mayo, you're in this thing way over your head. You're messing with dangerous people. Why not cut your losses and go back to doing cosy little insurance jobs?' English was giving nothing away.

'Why did you give me all that drivel about rape when the Coroner's report found no evidence of violence other than the stab wound?' I knew I wouldn't get an answer.

'Let me tell you what I think. We know Michelle is Barry Raphael's daughter who he hasn't seen for over twenty years. We also know that Darren Tonks, the late Darren Tonks, was Mick Raphael's son. Michelle and Darren shared the same mother. Now, I can't believe that Michelle coincidentally finds herself working at her long-lost father's gym. She deliberately gets herself a job there... Then something happens. Michelle has an affair with Paul Johnson and ends up dead in her car. There is no motive for Paul to kill her. If he did do the dirty deed, his track-covering skills are in dire need of sharpening up. Nobody is dumb enough to "hide" the murder weapon in their own work-locker. How am I doing?' I waited for a response.

'You're an intellectual midget, Mr Mayo. Stay with what you know best. Go and serve some process.' English gave me the sort of look which could turn milk sour.

I left the bedsit and returned to the office, where I typed up a brief letter on a piece of English's nicely embossed, headed notepaper. The gist of the letter was that English had been called abroad on urgent business and had made the necessary arrangements for Mr Jacobs to take over the Paul Johnson case. I returned to Ralph's bedsit, where English still had that look on his face.

'Sign this,' I said, giving him the letter and a pen.

'What is it?'

'A letter for the courts handing your Johnson case over to Noddy Jacobs.'

'Not a chance,' he smirked.

Ralph went across to a wardrobe with a squeaky door and took out an electric hammer-action drill. I watched him fit a tungsten bit and plug it into the wall-socket.

'Ralph, what are you doing?' I asked, thinking this was not the time to put up shelves.

'English is full of shit. I'm gonna drill a few holes in the guy to let some of it out.' He switched on the drill and upped the speed setting to High. Ralph walked across to English. The look on the lawyer's smug face dissolved into incredulity and then quickly into fear as Ralph brought the vibrating drill-bit dangerously close to his throat. English tried to back off but the bedpost prevented much movement.

'All right, you crazy bastards, I'll sign, I'll sign!' he screamed, as Ralph whisked past his throat and drilled a half-inch hole into the post. English signed the letter.

'Shove something back in his mouth, Ralph,' I said. 'I

don't care what it is.' I went back to the office, where Tess had fallen asleep on the floor. The first job of the morning would be to go and see Noddy Jacobs with English's letter. Paul Johnson was due to appear again before Lichfield Magistrates at ten a.m. and I wanted Noddy there, in court.

Ralph walked in and made some remark about Tess's bare backside, which was in plain view as she slept face down on the hard lino next to my desk, her head resting on her forearms. He studied her porcelain skin like you'd study a road map, before planting a sweet kiss on her rump.

'Can you transport English to your brother's place today without alerting the constabulary?' I asked him.

'No problem. I'll shove him in the boot. Tony's kids can play with him for a few days.'

Tess began to wake. She raised herself to a sitting position and rubbed the sleep from her eyes. Ralph went out to the Capri Café to get some food for us.

'Tess, I'm going to see Noddy Jacobs this morning. Paul's at Court and he can apply for bail.' I began to make three hot, tasteless drinks.

'I'll drive to Lichfield. I must see Paul. What can I wear, Jack? I can't turn up at Court in Ralph's pyjamas.'

'I'll go and see Diane, next door. She might have something you could borrow. You make the coffee.'

I went to Diane's Sauna. Diane had just arrived at work and found a size twelve black on white polka-dot dress with button front and a pair of size five flat black shoes, all from the locker of one of her girls. I promised to return the clothes and hurried back to the office.

Ralph had already started tucking into a mammoth sandwich of bacon, sausage and runny fried egg. The yolk dripped down his shirt. Tess brought over mugs of coffee and I handed her the dress and shoes. Without warning she pulled the baggy pyjama top over her head and stood before us, naked, as she undid the dozen or so buttons on the dress.

Ralph stopped chewing and sat, staring, open-mouthed. I could see the contents of his orifice and it wasn't something to send to the great memory bank of life.

'Who does the dress belong to, Jack?' Tess asked, totally at ease, her large breasts standing proud and firm. I looked at them for a moment before my eyes moved under the arch of her ribcage, down the flat of her stomach to the dark delta between her legs. She slipped the dress on but didn't fasten it, wearing it like a robe. Putting on the shoes she walked over to the small mirror on the wall near the tea-makings.

'Either of you got a comb?' she asked.

Ralph pulled out a black plastic one from his jacket pocket and passed it to Tess. It appeared to have fewer teeth than an inner-city pensioner. She tidied her blonde hair and handed the comb back to Ralph. It was then, and only then, that she decided to button up the dress. Ralph went back to his breakfast. The show was over.

'I'll drive us round in my car today, Jack,' Tess said, like I had any choice. I finished the coffee, took a few mouthfuls of Cheesy Vic's version of the sausage and tomato sandwich and followed Tess's shapely rear out to her car. After last night's thunderstorm, we were back to clear blue skies and sunshine. It felt crisper, much less humid than the previous few days. We'd arranged to see Ralph back at the office that afternoon.

Tess reversed her Mini across the pavement, scattering a bunch of taxi drivers chatting near the shattered glass of the bus shelter. She cut up a guy driving a Securicor van and raced through Birmingham's rush-hour traffic, giving scant regard to such things as 'right of way' and 'common courtesy'. By eight forty-five a.m. we were parked, just a few feet from the kerb, in Colmore Row. I made a donation to the City Council's coffers and, in return, got parking for an hour or so.

Noddy's office was on the third floor of a shabby,

rundown block in Church Street. The entrance hall still boasted a wall-plate for all the current tenants. It looked like it had last been updated about the same time the *Evening Despatch* ceased to be. We took the old, gated lift and walked down a dark corridor to the door marked *Nathan T. Jacobs, Solicitor*. There was no sign of life. At nine o'clock the lift whirred into action and halted at our floor. The gates clattered open and a red-faced Noddy Jacobs came hurrying down the hall towards us, carrying a large pile of paperwork wrapped in pink legal ribbon.

'Jack, old son, how are you?' Jacobs held out his chubby hand and I shook it.

'Fine. This is Mrs Johnson, Paul's wife,' I said.

'Charmed to meet you, my dear,' he said, kissing the back of her outstretched hand. 'Shall we go inside?'

He unlocked the door to his office suite. It looked like a cluster bomb had gone off inside but Noddy assured me he just worked that way. We declined his offer of a gin and tonic and handed him the letter signed by English.

'I'll have to go to Birmingham Magistrates' Court first to drop my workload there on somebody else. I'll phone Lichfield to let them know I'm on my way,' Jacobs said. I handed him the further paperwork we'd got from English and he promised to make an application for bail on Paul's behalf. Tess and I left him to drink his breakfast in peace.

'Jack, have you got any cash with you?' Tess asked.

'Just two fivers which are drying out, some change and my flexible friend. Why?'

'I need something to wear. If I can't get home then I must do some shopping.'

'We'll get you something in Lichfield,' I said, getting back into her car. Tess put a Lionel Ritchie tape into the stereo and we sped off.

Tess parked in the multi-storey car park off Birmingham Road, which was handy for the Magistrates' Court in Frog

Lane, and bought the requisite ticket. You could park forever in Lichfield for what you'd pay for an hour in Birmingham.

She then led me to a ladies' clothes shop in Market Street and we went inside. A woman of about forty wearing her hair in a trendy bob and her horn-rimmed glasses on a chain greeted us, speaking like she had somebody's plums in her mouth. Tess began looking at a rail of clothes while I stood nearby, wishing I were dead. A middle-aged woman in ridiculously tight white trousers and cowboy boots came into the shop with her husband, who wore a naff grey-leather bomber jacket over his beige Bermuda shorts, Argyll socks and open-toed sandals. They began examining the dresses in the section marked Sale.

'How about this one, Jack?' Tess shouted, holding up a salmon-pink dress with the sort of thin straps which she always had trouble with.

'Yeah, great,' I said, trying to hide my indifference.

'I'll try it on,' Tess added, walking off to the curtained changing cubicle. She came out wearing the pink dress which really suited her, twirled several times before the mirror and decided she'd take it. Tess walked back towards the cubicle, unzipping the back of the dress as she went. She stopped at the underwear display and picked up a pair of lacy black panties and a pair of pink court shoes, which she took back to the cubicle.

'I'll take them all,' she told the shop assistant, 'and I'll wear them.'

Tess came out of the cubicle carrying the polka dot dress and shoes she'd borrowed from the Sauna. The assistant held the price tag hanging from the dress strap, £29.99, and tapped it into the till. She looked at the shoes, compared them with similar pairs still on the rack, and tapped in £22.99 and then asked Tess what sort of panties she'd bought.

127

Tess hitched up her skirt to reveal a tiny black see-through G-string. The guy in the Bermuda shorts suddenly lost all interest in the Sale rack and cast his eyes over the curves of my client. Tess eventually located a price tag of £4.99, but not before the chap in the shorts took on the look of a man about to suffer a stroke. Tess smoothed down her dress and I handed over my plastic card. The shop assistant did the necessary and then snipped the tag from Tess's new dress. We left the store.

'Tess, can I use your car?' I asked. 'I want to visit the Raphaels again.' She handed me the keys, which I took to mean yes, and while she went on to the Magistrates' Court, I took her borrowed clothes back to the Mini and drove off in the direction of the Raphael household.

I felt it was time somebody started to tell me what the hell was going on: chez Raphael seemed as good a place as any to start. There were no cars parked on the gravel drive as I turned off the leafy lane. As a sign of respect, I parked on Barry's close-cropped lawn. I walked straight round the back to the poolside patio, but there were no naked girls frolicking in the pool today, which was a cause of some disappointment, and no sign of Barry Raphael, either. Instead, there was a woman in her mid-forties, in a fetching, one-piece black and jade swimsuit, cut high on the legs and low at the bosom. She had long ash-blonde hair and the sort of figure she'd clearly worked hard to achieve.

'Mrs Raphael?' I said. She was sprawled out on the same lounger Beverley had used a few days ago, and sipping something wet and red through a straw from a cocktail glass.

'You must be Jack Mayo,' she said. 'Barry told me you never ring the doorbell.'

'Sorry,' I said, 'but my command of Filipino leaves everything to be desired.' Talking of desire, I scanned her form with my eyes. She was the sort of sophisticated older woman you always hoped to meet as a randy eighteen-year-old. But never did.

'What do you want – may I call you Jack?' she enquired. Nice to see somebody in the Raphael camp had manners.

'Please do. I'd like to ask you a few questions concerning the murder of Michelle Rosa, Mrs Raphael.'

'Call me Helen,' she said, 'and you'd better pull up a seat.'

I dragged a garden chair across and sat close enough to smell her exquisite perfume and see the blue of her eyes.

'Let me get you a drink.' She stood up and walked across to the drinks trolley. 'Scotch okay?'

'Perfect,' I said, looking at her tanned body. She worked out, that's for certain. There was no flab, no cellulite, and you could probably have struck a match on her tight little ass. Helen returned with my whisky and, after handing it over, lay back on the lounger. I took a gulp.

'What can you tell me about Michelle Rosa?' I asked.

'She worked as an aerobics instructor at my husband's gym in Lichfield. I believe she was very good at her job. I found out yesterday that she was Barry's daughter from his first marriage.'

'Did that bother you?'

'Not at all. As a matter of fact, it quite cheered me up.'

'What do you mean?' I asked, simultaneously looking at her tanned, freckly breasts. She didn't seem to mind.

'Until Barry told me that Michelle was his daughter, I had a horrible nagging feeling that he was somehow mixed up in her death. I'm quite certain, Jack, that even my husband wouldn't kill his own child.'

'I know this may sound personal, but what sort of a relationship do you and your husband enjoy?'

She smiled. There was a slight, very slight gap between her two upper front teeth. I noticed she wore red lipstick and a little eye shadow. Only the laughter lines around her eyes gave away her age. I couldn't imagine she developed them around Raphael.

'Ours isn't so much an open marriage, Jack, it's bloody windswept,' she laughed. 'Physically we lost interest in each other years ago.'

'What do you get out of it?' I asked.

'Look around you. A big, Grade Two listed house, several acres of land, a swimming pool, a Mercedes Sports in the garage, wardrobes full of designer clothes and a monthly allowance from Barry of ten thousand pounds. Does that answer your question?'

I smiled and took a mouthful of scotch. It tasted like a good malt. Only the best for the Raphaels.

'Do you use the gym at all?' I continued.

'Yes, regularly. I also have a personal trainer visit me here twice a week. I like to keep in shape.'

'You've managed that, all right,' I said.

'Thank you, Jack. That's kind of you.'

'Do you know the staff at the gym?' I wanted some background on Barry's employees.

'Of course. Beverley Calvert, Vanessa Lewis, Errol, the black hunk, Cain Netto, my personal trainer. I know them all very well. Barry knows some of them even better, if you catch my drift. Inside out, as it were.'

'Cain Netto,' I mused. 'Is that a man or a woman?'

Helen giggled. 'He's a man, silly. He has a body any woman would kill for. Sorry, that's a bad phrase to use in the circumstances. He is muscular and handsome, with long flowing locks. He's my Tarzan, Jack. He works my body, in more ways than one.'

The picture she painted was an artist's impression of the git who had tried to introduce lead to my diet, out on the muddy wasteland.

'How well do you know Eddie English?' I changed tack.

'Very well. He's been Barry's solicitor for many years, and often comes here for social occasions. Why?'

'I just wondered why he would end up representing Paul Johnson, when Paul had allegedly just murdered Barry's daughter.'

'You must understand, Jack, that my husband's background is, shall we say, a little tarnished. He wanted a speedy end to the whole affair. The police caught Paul and charged him, so Barry sent Eddie to act as Paul's defence. Apart from anything else, it meant Barry knew exactly what was happening in the case all the time. There's nothing sinister about that.'

'When did your husband find out Michelle was his daughter? And *how* did he find out?'

'He didn't tell me and I didn't ask. It's a part of his life I have no involvement in.'

'Do you know where Michelle lived?' I asked, setting down the empty glass on the floor.

'She shared a flat with Vanessa Lewis. Beverley jokes that they are – or were, I should say – lesbians.'

'Where does this Vanessa live?'

'Number fourteen, Boswell House. It's near Stowe Pool in Lichfield. My husband helped her find the deposit for her mortgage then helped her find her G spot.' She lowered the lounger to the full horizontal position and turned over. The bathing costume was cut low at the back.

'Be an absolute angel, Jack, and smooth some of that lotion on my back and shoulders.'

I could spare a couple of minutes. I squeezed a handful of Piz Buin into the palm of my left hand and began applying it to Mrs Raphael's back. She'd closed her eyes. I worked the sticky cream into her firm skin, which was already brown, pulled down the straps to do her shoulders, then replaced the bottle. I left without saying another word.

*

I knew Vanessa would be at work at the gym, so I felt it was the ideal time to go to her flat. I parked Tess's Mini under a footbridge in Stowe Road, and jogged round to nearby Boswell House. It was one of those flat-roofed jobs which architects disfigured our cities with in the sixties. Number 14 was on the ground floor of a four-storey block. I put my weight to the flimsy front door and gained immediate access. There was nobody else about and I felt safe for a few minutes. It was a one-bedroomed flat, furnished, no doubt, with more than a little of Uncle Barry's hard-extorted cash. I felt the adjustable Weider weightlifting bench in the lounge was a little out of place, as was the chinning bar fitted across the doorframe of the kitchen. Dozens of glossy weightlifting magazines were scattered around, most featuring muscle-men in ripped Gold's Gym vests lifting scantily-clad young women. What a way to make a living!

There were photographs on the walls and standing on the sideboard and table. Most featured Vanessa in her various poses and costumes. I opened the drawer of the sideboard and found two albums of photographs. One contained more pictures of Vanessa posing, or taking part in body-building competitions; some showed her working out. There was one of her hugging Barry Raphael after apparently winning a competition.

I opened the other album. The photographs inside weren't of Vanessa but of another girl. A girl with light brown hair, blue eyes and the face of a schoolgirl on the body of an adult woman. I wondered if this could be Michelle. None of the pictures had captions or dates. I turned the pages and the girl went from posing in her aerobic kit to posing with no kit. The pictures became more daring as she posed topless, then full-frontal. Then the pictures switched to what looked like the inside of a bedroom, but not the one in the flat. These were still photographs of a man and a woman making love. Making love in various positions. Making love wearing leather or nothing at all. The woman was the same as before. Possibly Michelle Rosa. I recognised the man. It was Barry Raphael.

CHAPTER 9

I put the album down where I'd remember to pick it up and continued searching the flat. I went through to the bedroom. Double bed, in antique pine. Gold satin sheets. Some nice, sexy lingerie in her chest of drawers but nothing of any note. Photos of bodybuilders on the walls, mostly women. Posters of Cory Everson, captioned *Ms Olympia*, which was very politically correct, I thought.

I moved to the bathroom, which was finished in avocado. I opened an avocado cupboard and found several boxes of tablets, marked STANOZOLOL. There was a pamphlet alongside the tablets titled *Anabolic Steroids*. It didn't take me long to realise what the tablets were and when I'd finished reading the pamphlet I knew why Vanessa was taking them.

Anabolic steroids were used by athletes, especially bodybuilders, to promote rapid muscle growth. They were banned by the IAAF way back in 1970 but it never stopped their use. The tablets, in pop-out foil, were in 5 mg doses which was, according to the instructions, the regular daily amount.

The pamphlet went on to talk about the various side-effects. These included, obviously, the development of bigger muscles. In women, facial hair would start to grow in some cases. They could even develop male pattern baldness, and their vocal chords could lengthen, causing their voices to break. I found it more interesting to note that women who took anabolic steroids could find their sexual appetites increase. The reverse was the case with men taking steroids. Women were also prone to develop masculine features, and hypertrophy of the clitoris was common, sometimes embarrassingly so. The sage who had written the papers rabbited on about how steroids built bigger muscles but actually added nothing to a person's strength. By all accounts the Home Office was considering adding anabolic steroids to the Misuse of Drugs Act. That consideration started in September 1987 and was still ongoing: the Home Office hates to be rushed. I put the tablets and pamphlet back, picked up the album and hurriedly left the flat, pulling the front door to after me. You can't be too careful, these days.

I drove back to Lichfield and picked up Tess from outside the Courts. We swapped seats and she drove us back to the office.

'How did you get on?' I asked.

'Paul's still in custody for another seven days. You just missed Noddy. He said he'd ring you later. Noddy at least persuaded Paul to stay with his plea of Not Guilty. He's very down, Jack.'

Tess seemed equally depressed and we barely spoke again. She parked close to the glass-free bus shelter and we climbed out. I clocked that there were two bodies in our doorway. One, as ever, belonged to Claude. The other belonged to the big ugly thug who tried to light my blue-touch paper with the unfortunate Norman Paget. He appeared comatose. Maybe Claude's taken a lodger, I thought, stepping over the bodies, and helping Tess do the same.

Ralph was on the phone when we pushed the office door open. The remains of a wooden chair littered the floor.

'I told you, Tony, if he gets gobby give him a dig. He's only a bleedin' solicitor. Get your missus to sit on his face or something. Yeah, okay. See you later.' Ralph put down the phone.

'Hi, Jack. Tess,' he said, lighting up a Panatella with his KKE Greek Communist Party plastic lighter.

'What the hell happened, Ralph?' I felt obliged to ask.

'You mean the ape downstairs? He came in half an hour ago and started throwing his weight around. So I gave him a hand and threw his weight out of the office and down the stairs. His name's Al Savage, according to the UB40 card in his pocket. A very apt name, given his line of work. What did he want? Came looking for Eddie. I'll phone the public works department and get him shifted.'

'Paul's still in custody, as we expected. At least he's pleading Not Guilty now. I went across to Raphael's place. He was out but his wife was there. She was okay. Forthcoming, but then she didn't know very much. What she did give me was Vanessa's address in Lichfield.'

'Vanessa?' Ralph asked.

'Pay attention, Ralph. She's one of Raphael's floosies. She works as a trainer at his gym and shared her flat with Michelle. I went over there and found out she's on anabolic steroids, which may or may not be of importance, and I also found this.' I threw the heavy, green-covered photo album onto Ralph's desk, disturbing his dust collection.

He opened it and looked at the various pictures. 'Who's the bird Raphael's humping?' he asked.

'I don't know. I think it might be Michelle Rosa.'

'His daughter?' Tess asked.

'The very same,' I replied.

'I'm getting more and more confused, Jack. I've got a tense, nervous headache.' Ralph scratched his bonce.

'I've been thinking about this all the way back from Lichfield. Supposing the photos are of Michelle. She's a fit, attractive girl of twenty-four who just happens to carry the burden of a deep hatred for her father around with her. He

136

dumped her and Mum when she was just a toddler. Mum went on the game and life turned to faeces before her very eyes. So she plots revenge. She knows she has to get Barry bang to rights, get him once and for all, and she also knows his one soft spot is anything with a pretty face. Michelle's got a pretty face. *Had* a pretty face. She gets a job at his gym knowing that, with his reputation, it's only a matter of time before he invites himself into her scanty panties. Michelle leads him on a treat and they bonk themselves stupid. At some point she gets their antics on film, maybe even a video. Then she whispers sweet somethings into Raphael's ear, like "You've been shafting your own daughter for the last two weeks and now I'm going to the law." Raphael knows he's done for: he can pull seven years for incest. So he decides, daughter or not, that Michelle's got to go. Of course, he doesn't carry out the dreadful deed himself. He gets a paid stooge to do that – probably Errol or the hairy git. Maybe even the big fool downstairs. Then they needed a sucker to set up. Barry learns that Paul is poking Michelle – forgive my terminology, Tess,' I said.

'It all amounts to the same thing, Jack, whichever way you say it. I can't blame him, she was a very attractive girl.' She had taken the news with a certain style, I thought.

'So Barry finds out Paul's seeing Michelle and, bingo! He's got a purpose-built victim. What he ain't got, with Paul, is a motive. So Eddie English comes along and the next thing you know Paul's changing his plea to Guilty. Why? 'Cos he's been got at, maybe threatened: "Change your plea or we kill your wife." Maybe bribes: "You plead Guilty to a lousy manslaughter, do your time and Mr Raphael will send a couple of hundred grand your way." Maybe a bit of both – same threat, same bribe.'

'It all sounds very good, Jack, but we can't prove any of it,' Ralph said, blowing foul-smelling smoke at me.

'If we can identify the girl in the photographs as Michelle, then we can prove Raphael's incestuous affair. If nothing else, it would cast enough doubt over Michelle's death to get Paul released. I'll take a photo to Lichfield Police station if I get the chance and speak to one of the cops on the case. They saw her body, maybe they'll identify her.'

'What about the steroids?' asked Tess.

'Probably Errol or his pal were pushing them at the gym.'

'Ralph, I think we need to pay Eddie a brief visit,' I said. We left Tess at the office and went down to the Allegro. The big dummy had taken the hint and left the scene. Ralph drove us to his brother's ground-floor maisonette in a rundown part of Nechells.

At least four windows at the flat had been smashed and repaired with cardboard. It looked like a stationery warehouse from the outside. The curtains and nets resembled rags used to clean the grime off buses. There was plastic carpet protector underfoot, but no carpet. It smelt as if Koreans had moved in and cooked stray dogs.

Eddie was handcuffed to a copper boiler in an empty bedroom. Ralph told me later that Tony did a bit of tatting and the boiler would have come from a void flat somewhere locally. Eddie had felt-tip pen marks on his face, courtesy of Tony's two kids. He looked a little down in the dumps. He *was* down in a dump, come to think of it.

'Eddie, you're lookin' good! Day-glo yellow really suits you,' I said, referring to the marks on his cheeks.

'Get me out of this shit-hole, Mayo,' English whined.

'Then talk to me, Eddie,' I said.

'I can't, Mayo. You know I can't.'

'Fair enough. Let me talk to you and you just nod your head if I'm right.' I sat on the floor next to English, stretching out my legs and putting the weight on my palms. 'We know that Michelle Rosa was Barry Raphael's daughter – correct?'

English nodded.

'We believe he had an affair with Michelle and she threatened to blow the whistle. A different sort of blow-job for a change . . . When Raphael found out he'd be up on an incest charge he arranged for Michelle to be snotted. How am I doing?' I asked.

English looked at me for a moment or two, then spoke.

'Barry Raphael didn't know Michelle from Adam when she got a job at the gym as aerobics instructor. She was properly qualified. She made a play for Barry and he couldn't resist. As far as he was concerned she was just another lovely woman to screw. They had sex regularly and then, one night in bed, she told him the awful truth: he'd been having sexual intercourse with his own flesh and blood. She told him that there were photographs and even a video which she'd set up with a friend whilst they had a dirty weekend in London. Michelle gave Barry one of the photographs. She told him she was going to the police to have him charged with incest. She also told him he'd be looking at seven years on conviction. The girl had done her homework, but not quite as thoroughly as she should. To secure a conviction, it was necessary to prove that Raphael *knew* Michelle was his daughter. Plainly he did not and he was rather relieved when I told him. There was never any necessity for Barry to kill Michelle or have her killed, for that matter. You're barking up the wrong family tree, Mayo. You've drawn a blank.'

I got up and left the room. We were suddenly back to square one and I'd lost the dice. I found Ralph playing with his eight-year-old nephew, Sebastian, and told him we were going. On the way out to the rusting Allegro, Ralph made a grunting noise and expelled the contents of each nostril in turn onto the pavement. This was the sort of neighbourhood where local etiquette wouldn't be offended.

'Now where, Jack?' he asked.

'That's a good question, Ralph. A damn good question.'

Ralph conveyed me to the office, then went on to see Maggie for an ID on the girl in the sexy photographs. Tess was making herself useful by filing her fingernails. She could sense things hadn't gone well.

'Jack, what is it? What's wrong?' she enquired.

'It's that obvious, is it? English pulled the rug from under our incest idea. I'm beginning to think we'll never get to the bottom of this case, Tess. It'll turn up in mystery books alongside the *Mary Celeste* and the Bermuda Triangle.'

'Don't give up, please, Jack.' She looked directly into my eyes and touched my hand. 'Why don't we call it a day? I'm working at the Viking tonight. Maybe things will seem clearer in the morning.'

I found enough motivation to nod my head and we locked up the office. Tess drove me home and dropped me off at the end of my street. Things, I thought, couldn't get much worse.

As it transpired, things could get quite a bit worse. I went indoors to find a scribbled note from my wife saying she'd taken the kids and gone to stay with her parents in Burnham-On-Sea. Her parents were the only people in the northern hemisphere without a telephone. I picked up the post from the last few days and discovered bills for gas and water rates and the usual junk mail. I slumped into an armchair with a can of lager and dozed off.

Somebody rapping on the front door woke me up. I ignored the knocking but the caller was persistent. I was in just the right mood for Jehovah's Witnesses, but on opening the door I found myself face to face with Detective Constable Eric Pillinger, of Cheapside CID. An ex-colleague. A talentless prat. With him was an attached bobby in the jacket of one suit and the trousers of another. Pillinger held up his black leather warrant card, like we'd never met before.

'Detective Sergeant Pillinger,' he said. 'Cheapside CID. This is Temporary Detective Constable Strong. Can we come in, please?'

'Is this a social call, Eric?' I asked.

'I'm afraid not, Jack. You're under arrest on suspicion of murder.'

'Have you gone fuckin' ga-ga?' I felt obliged to ask.

'This isn't a joke,' he replied.

'You'd better come in. Refresh my memory, Eric. Who did I murder?'

'A lad by the name of Darren Michael Tonks. You don't mind if DC Strong searches your house, do you?'

'I know I've no choice. Where are you taking me?'

'Cheapside,' Pillinger said, gesturing to Strong to get cracking on the search. Pillinger joined the job about four years ago and was quickly earmarked for promotion. A graduate entrant, he was a complete and utter waste of space. I guessed he was about nine stones, wet through, with a neck like a cheap biro. His shirt collars were always too big. He'd come in really useful at a pub fight, holding the jackets.

'I don't want to sound didactic, Eric, old son, but when were you thinking of cautioning me?' I hoped my smirk was noticeable.

Pillinger coughed, then said, 'You don't have to say anything unless you wish to do so but what you say may be used in evidence.'

'It's a fair cop, guv. There, I've always wanted to say that. Make sure you remember that. The Uzi is in the tumble dryer, by the way.'

'You won't be laughing later, Mayo,' Pillinger said, somewhat threateningly.

'I can't believe you're a Sergeant, Pillinger, and a Detective Sergeant to boot. Still, at least it explains the scratching noises I heard. It was West Midlands Police scraping the bottom of the barrel to promote you. I bet you're really popular in the office.'

Strong returned from his search with nothing.

'I'll be checking my wife's panty drawer later, to make sure there's none missing,' I said, by way of light relief.

'I hope there's no need for handcuffs, Mayo,' Pillinger said.

'Did you come on your own? I expected you at least to have a vanload of riot police. You've gone up in my estimation, Pillinger. Not that you could go in any other direction, you understand.'

I was led outside to the white Maestro CID car and put in the rear nearside seat, as per the training manual. Pillinger sat alongside me and Strong drove. No words were exchanged on the way to Cheapside nick. Strong parked in the police bay and Pillinger took my right arm and led me inside. We went through the coded front door and then through a similar door into the custody suite. 'Custody suite' . . . who on earth came up with *that* misnomer!

Pillinger led me to the black-topped charge counter where a uniformed sergeant was filling in an old person-in-custody sheet. He ignored Pillinger, as most people tend to do. The arresting officer cleared his throat by way of announcing his presence. The custody sergeant, a rotund guy with grey hair and bushy sideburns, looked up.

'When I'm good and ready,' he said to Pillinger, and carried on with what he was doing. I looked around the place I used to work in. Nothing had changed. Same fleck-painted walls, same wipe-clean board with prisoner details marked on it, same yellowing reports hanging on the walls. Same panic alarm system. People were coming and going throughout the cell block. It was a busy, City Centre station. A young uniformed officer hovered in the background with a handful of paperwork and a smarmy-looking defence brief. A young WPC arrived with a mug of tea for the harassed desk sergeant and an old pal of mine, Detective Constable Tim O'Rourke, came into the block with a blue charge sheet to pin to the PIC sheet of some other sucker in custody. Judging from the number of PIC sheets arranged lovingly across the counter, it was a busy day.

'Jack, what are you doing here?' Tim asked. He'd worked in the same CID office as me for a couple of years, but on a different crew. He was a good bobby, very thorough, but a family man. Family men don't get on in the police. You've got to be a piss-head and be seen to be a piss-head. One of the lads. Like Ralph, I suppose.

'I'm helping Silly Bollocks here with his enquiries. Somebody's got to, he screws 'em up on his own.' I grinned. Pillinger shifted uncomfortably from one foot to the other.

'You're pulling my pud. Under arrest – what for?' O'Rourke looked gob-smacked.

'Apparently I murdered somebody. The redoubtable Eric will furnish me with full and proper details in due course.'

'I don't know what to say, Jack,' Tim said, before dissolving in a fit of giggles. 'Wait till the lads hear of this.'

The custody sergeant looked up. 'Right. Next,' he said, in a gruff Glaswegian accent.

'I've arrested this man on suspicion of murder, Sergeant,' Pillinger said, 'at seventeen oh-five hours at his home address.'

'What's your name, son?' the sergeant asked, as he began to fill in another, fresh custody record. His handwriting looked like a cross between general practitioner and Linear B.

'John Patrick Mayo. Born 24 July 1955, Birmingham. I'm a Leo,' I said, as a start.

'Empty your pockets onto the desk, Jack,' Pillinger said. I was still wearing the clothes Ralph had lent me. The pockets were all empty.

'I travel light,' I said.

'I'll take the belt,' Pillinger said, pointing at the cheap canvas belt holding up the jeans. 'I wouldn't want you doing anything stupid.'

'No,' I smiled, 'you've got the monopoly on that.'

I gave the custody sergeant my address and inside leg measurement and asked him to contact Noddy Jacobs as my mouthpiece. Pillinger then had a brainwave and decided to seize my clothes as evidence, for forensic analysis. I didn't have the heart to tell him that the clothes weren't mine and, in any case, I wasn't wearing them when Darren flew through the air with the greatest of ease. He handed me a zip-up hooded suit made of white paper, for use in such cases. I often wondered why the suits had hoods, since they were only worn in the cell area. He put the red polo shirt, jeans, socks and trainers in individual brown paper bags and carefully labelled them. Ralph would be really impressed to know that half his wardrobe was en route to the forensic lab.

I signed the PIC sheet as correct and Pillinger led me through the cell passage. He opened up the solid door of the second cell along with one of a dozen heavy keys on a ring and chain.

'I'll speak to you later,' he said, slamming the door and closing the trap. I turned round to locate the source of the repulsive stench occupying my nostrils and saw a drunk dressed in a Combat Johnny outfit lying in the recovery position on the built-in wooden bench. He was snoring and being generally annoying. I relocated him to the floor and covered him with an old Army blanket. I looked at the loo in the corner and saw it was in dire need of flushing. Since the chain was in the cell passage to prevent prisoners ending it all, at least by chain, I had to put up with it. I reclined on the bench and stared at the cream-painted brick wall.

I began to think about Ralph and our days together during the miners' strike in 1984. On one occasion we were based at a military camp near Grantham and every morning we'd be ferried to the colliery at Blidworth. You could always tell West Midlands bobbies in those days. No two cops had the same style macs or overcoats. One older guy even had a cape. We were transported by a civilian driver in a hired coach. Other forces turned up in smart uniforms, all matching, and properly kitted out police transit vans with full riot protection.

Ralph became notorious for his nocturnal habits. There were over a hundred policemen billeted in a gymnasium, sleeping on camp beds. Some worked mornings, some days, some nights. It meant you never got to sleep because of the noise of people walking about, chatting and using electric shavers. It was Hell Week. Ralph took to getting pissed each night in the NAAFI then relieving himself either in somebody's locker or over some sleeping cop from somewhere like Cheshire. One guy complained and later reported sick. He was overcome by the fumes from Ralph's urine.

Ralph has his good side, though. I remember an old dear being robbed in the Bull Ring one Sunday morning after going to church. A yob snatched her handbag and sent the pensioner spinning to the subway floor. He got away with her life savings of over a thousand pounds. The lady told Ralph that she felt it was unsafe to leave the money at home. Ralph immediately organised a whip-round amongst the lads on the shift and anybody else he could find. He gave twenty quid himself and helped raise over two hundred pounds for the lady. That was two hundred quid more than she got from her church. No wonder they're all soddin' empty. The culprit was never caught.

The smell of the drunk in the corner of my cell was making me sick. There is no smell on earth as bad as a stale drunk with criminal body odour. This chap could make a skunk curl up and die.

I dozed off, only to be woken by the rattling of the keys in the door. The Custody Officer stood there with Noddy Jacobs. Noddy wore a turquoise bow tie and a shirt that was frayed at the collar. The custody sergeant sprayed the room with fresh air spray and Noddy ventured in.

'Now what have you done, Jack?' he asked.

'Detective Sergeant Pillinger is of the opinion that I killed a glue-sniffer called Darren Tonks. He's wrong, of course, but he does insist on formally interviewing me and formally making a complete prat of himself.'

'What are the circs?'

'Last Tuesday afternoon I went to the lad's address. He lives on the fifteenth floor – *lived* on the fifteenth floor, I should say – of a high-rise slum in Newtown. Darren was the step-brother or half-brother of Michelle Rosa, the murder victim in the Paul Johnson case. With me so far? In between inhaling glue fumes from a plastic bag, Darren gave me a little information. I don't think he trusted me, being an ex-cop. The next morning I called to see him again. I got as far as the car park and saw the police and ambulance guys there. Darren had fallen to his untimely death. I didn't think then that he'd jumped or slipped. Somebody helped him on his way.'

'Why does Pillinger think it was you?' Noddy enquired.

'On the basis that my business card was found in Darren's pocket and a uniformed cop clocked me at the scene.'

'How do you want to play this, Jack? A No Comment interview?'

'No. Pillinger might think he's onto a winner. I'll answer his questions. If he charges me with murder, he's an even bigger fool than I already take him for.'

We called the custody officer and he led us back to the charge office, where Pillinger and Strong were waiting, armed with brand new cassette tapes and paperwork. Noddy and I went into the interview room, which measured about ten feet by ten feet. A square, teak-effect table on black, tubular steel legs was set against the far wall. There were five plastic, stackable chairs arranged haphazardly around the room. A black Neal tape recorder with two decks sat on the table. The room was lit by fluorescent light and the walls were clad with grey-green acoustic tiles. The air-conditioner whirred overhead.

I took a chair at the table and Noddy sat alongside me. He took a writing pad and pencil from his battered black briefcase. Pillinger sat down opposite me and Strong alongside him. I watched the detective sergeant unwrap the two blank cassettes and place one in each of the decks. He pressed the red 'record' button and sat forward in his seat.

'This interview is being conducted in an interview room at Cheapside Police Station. I am Detective Sergeant Pillinger and also present are . . .' Pillinger looked at his colleague.

'PC Strong.' Good, clear voice.

'Jack Mayo, private detective and sexual athlete,' I said.

'Mr Jacobs, solicitor,' Noddy muttered.

'Can I just confirm that there is nobody else present, Mr Mayo?' Pillinger said.

'Yeah. Get on with it, Pillinger, I've got a date tonight,' I said, trying to piss him off.

'The time is eighteen thirty-two hours on Friday sixteenth June 1992. I have to remind you, Mr Mayo, that you're still under caution. At the end of this interview you'll be given a form which outlines how you and your brief can get a copy of this interview tape. Right, do you understand why you've been arrested?' Pillinger sat back in his seat expecting a lengthy reply.

'Yeah,' I said, disappointingly.

'Tell me about it in your own words,' he said.

'I'm here to answer your questions,' I said, 'not give a speech.' He looked rather flummoxed.

'Er . . . how long have you know Darren Tonks?' he asked.

147

'Approximately twenty minutes,' I grinned. 'Met him at his flat on Tuesday afternoon.'

'For what reason?'

'He's related to a case I'm working on. He gave me some information.'

'We found your business card in his pocket,' Pillinger said.

'So what? If you'd found a note saying, "two extra pintas" would you have locked up the milkman?'

'I'll ask the questions. You still haven't explained why you called to see Tonks.'

'I went to invite him to a cheese, wine and adhesive party.'

At this Strong snorted, as if he was bursting to laugh. Pillinger gave him a look which said, 'Back in uniform for you, pal.'

'Why did you return there the following morning?' he asked.

'To return his copy of Moriarty's *Police Law* which he kindly lent me.'

'Mayo, don't mess about. Answer the questions. The sooner you answer them, the sooner you get to go home.'

'Okay. He invited me for a coffee morning. He's a good conversationalist and we planned to discuss the growing unrest in Azerbaijan and maybe sniff a little Bostik.'

'I think you killed him, Mayo.' Pillinger sat forwards again. It's about as near to intimidation as he gets.

'You probably think the earth is flat, Pillinger. Listen, if I had decided to throw the twerp out of his window I'd have waited until your car was parked underneath. You still driving that 2CV in British racing green? It's not a good car for somebody with your dynamism. Can I go now? I'm bored.'

'You'll go when I say so. If you're withholding information, Mayo, I'll see you get done for obstructing a police officer in the execution of his duty.'

148

'You're a real card, Pillinger. You arrest me for murder then threaten me with an obstruction charge. Your interviewing technique sucks like a thirty-bob whore. You know, the thought of a ponce like your good self running a police force in ten years' time scares the life out of me. You still married to that leftie bint?'

Pillinger was married to a woman, a teacher, whose politics were to the left of the Redgraves. She wore clothes from Oxfam shops and had her hair styled, or so it looked, by a combine harvester. She drank Nicaraguan coffee and called herself a vegan. Vegan is just a posh way of saying hunger-striker in my book.

'Why won't you talk to me, Jack?' Pillinger asked.

'Because you're a know-nothing shite. A decent cop would have arranged to meet me in a pub and asked me these questions over a pint and a pie. A decent cop would have got all the answers. Not you. You've got to do it all by the book and embarrass me in front of my old colleagues. And it's got you nowhere.'

I could have told him to liaise with the police in Lichfield as Darren's death tied in with Michelle's. I could have. I didn't.

'Anything else you want to say?' he asked.

'Nope.'

'This interview is terminated. The time is eighteen thirty-eight hours. I am now switching off the tape.' Pillinger hit the grey stop button and removed both tapes. He labelled them up and I signed the self-adhesive labels. Darren could have sniffed them if he'd been there.

'I'm gonna bail you under Section 47(3) of the Bail Act to return to this police station in a month's time pending further enquiries. You can go. PC Strong will make the arrangements.'

'What about the clothing seized?' I asked.

'I'm keeping that until my enquiries are complete,'

149

Pillinger said, leaving the room a broken man. 'You can keep the paper suit,' he added, as a parting shot.

'If I get a spare moment, I'll write my confession on it,' I said, smiling. 'Any chance of a lift home, Noddy?'

Noddy lent me the cab-fare to Chasetown and I went straight home and got changed. I put on a petrol-blue casual shirt, a freshly cleaned pair of blue jeans and my brown leather moccasins. I'd spent the taxi journey mulling over the whole messy business, and the germ of an idea had emerged from the dark, damp recesses of my warped mind. I should have poured disinfectant over it. Instead, I phoned my mate Ralph.

CHAPTER 10

Ralph answered the blower in the office and I told him to call his brother to release English. I couldn't see any point in detaining Eddie any longer. Ralph promised he'd do it before the next World Cup Finals. I hoped he was joking.

'Ralph,' I said, picturing him in my mind's eye with his index finger inserted in a nostril, 'I'm gonna try and track down the kids who found Michelle's body. Maybe she said something interesting before she croaked. It's Saturday tomorrow. There's a chance they'll be back at Chasewater with their rods.'

'I thought I might drive across to the Viking. Tess is working tonight. It'll do me good to see some female flesh. Shall I pick you up?' Ralph didn't need to persuade me.

'All right. About ten o'clock?' I said.

'See you later.'

I slept on the sofa for a couple of hours before Ralph woke me up, banging on the door. He was suitably attired in a cream, short-sleeve shirt which was being asked to stretch too far across his beer gut, causing gaping holes between the buttons, trousers in the shade of brown normally monopolised by dog turds, and tan brogue shoes. He looked a million lire.

I got into the passenger seat of Ralph's state of the art

Allegro and clunk-clicked the seat belt. 'How's things?' he asked.

'The wife and kids have left me, Ralph. And this afternoon I got arrested for murder by the impressive Detective Sergeant Pillinger of Cheapside Police. Other than that, it's been quiet.'

'English is on the loose again. Tony dropped him off in a lay-by on the A38 near Sutton. He kept his shoes as a memento, though,' Ralph almost looked ashamed to say it, 'and his socks.'

We got to the pub at about ten-fifteen. Ralph made his way to the bar and returned to where I stood, near the nudge machine, with two pints of Banks's mild. I don't drink mild but I didn't want to hurt his feelings. He'd bought two tickets for the strip show.

Ralph kept me amused with an interminable joke about a nun and a cruise-missile-shaped vibrator before I talked him through my arrest. His only comment was a derogatory one which made specific reference to Pillinger's choice of sexual partner, namely his right hand.

The sandy-haired fellah was there to clear off the bona fide drinkers at eleven and usher the strip audience into the lounge bar. The curtains were drawn and the doors locked. I thought there were more punters than on the previous occasion. Ralph disagreed.

'Ladies and gentlemen, unfortunately Theresa cannot be with us tonight but I know you'll get just as big a kick out of her replacement. Please give a warm welcome to Nadine . . .'

The MC started the applause. I looked at Ralph, who shrugged his shoulders and drained his beer.

Heavy rock music came on, abruptly, and the curtain was drawn back. Whoever Nadine was, she was done up like a motorcycle courier, dressed from head to boots in biker gear. She was at least six feet tall. When she took off the laminated fibreglass helmet, she exposed a short, boyish hairstyle in peroxide blonde; her dark brown eyebrows revealed her true hair colour. She was attractive, with chocolate brown eyes and long lashes. Her lips were full, like a woman's lips should be, and her skin lightly tanned.

Ralph said he'd like to 'give her one' which I took to be his seal of approval. He rarely ventures such an opinion without first seeing the whole of the goods on offer. The stripper began pulsating her body in time with the rock backing track, something by REO Speedwagon, I think. She unbuckled the belt around the waist of her short, black leather jacket and slowly took it off, first from one shoulder, then the other. Finally she tossed the jacket to a bearded biker stood near the curtain. I guessed he was her minder. He was too butch to be a make-up artist.

Nadine unzipped her biker boots and eased them off before opening the press stud at the top of her black leather trousers with cute padded knees. Ralph said they'd be good for gardening, too. She unzipped the strides and inched them over her golden thighs, thighs which seemed never-ending. She stepped out of the trousers and kicked them to the hairy one, who looked like he'd attended to his hair with a rake.

Now Nadine stood in the centre of the room wearing only a black leather waistcoat and matching leather thong. You'd probably describe her as 'statuesque', always supposing you could still use such words after four pints of beer. She reminded me of the picture of the big girl on the wall of the Amazon Gym. Nadine was a true Amazon. She was the sort of girl you couldn't contemplate having sex with, without a safety net and a State Registered Nurse on stand-by. I watched her buttocks squeeze together as she moved around the clearing. There was no fat on her. This girl looked after her body. She began unbuttoning the waistcoat, slowly, suggestively, from the bottom upwards, before revealing two, huge tanned breasts to the incredulous men in the audience. The pink areolas covered areas which would normally require planning permission, and her nipples were like the tops of two Tipp-Ex bottles. Somebody at the back of the room was clearly so overcome as to drop his glass on the floor. The smashing noise was even louder for the room was, otherwise, silent. Even the rock music had finished, as Nadine began fondling her own bosom. Then, in a flash, she let her thong fall to the worn carpet and stood naked before the sort of cheers normally reserved for Cup Final Captains as they hoist the FA Cup above their heads. I studied her naked body and committed it to memory. Those magnificent mammaries. That dark, mysterious delta of pubic hair. The curves of her buttocks. A six-feet-tall blonde Aryan. Hitler would have loved her.

'I'm going to see Tess, Ralph. Can I borrow your motor car?' I was talking whilst watching Nadine's shapely rear disappear behind the curtain.

'Sure,' he said, handing me the keys. 'You don't mind if I stay and watch the show, do you?'

I grinned. 'No. I'll come back and pick you up.'

I started the Allegro by using plenty of choke and headed off to Tess's home. I was relieved to see she was in. I was relieved to see she was unharmed, and I was *very* relieved to see she was wearing a short, ivory-satin wrap with a floral print. She'd been crying again. Her eyes were red and puffy and she was holding the remains of a Kleenex in her right hand.

'Oh Jack, I'm so glad you're here,' she sighed, closing the door behind me. I followed her into the lounge where she'd been keeping company with a bottle of Stolichnaya vodka.

'What's the matter, honey?' I asked, trying to sound professional as my eyes drifted towards where her breasts were vying for pole position in the race to leave her wrap.

I poured myself a vodka without being asked and sat on

one of two identical sofas, facing each other across a mahogany coffee table. Tess sat on the other, tucking her legs beneath her and leaning on the polished wooden sofa arm.

'I had a visit earlier, from Helen Raphael – Barry's wife. She came here alone and offered me fifty thousand pounds immediately if I persuaded Paul to plead Guilty to a manslaughter charge, and a further one hundred thousand pounds for each year he serves in prison. I'm so confused, Jack. I don't know what to do.'

'It's a lot of money, Tess,' I said.

'She was very convincing. She said to tell Paul to treat his prison sentence like he was working abroad. She reckoned if somebody offered him a couple of hundred grand to spend two years laying sewers in some Third World doss-hole, he'd do it, so what's the difference? She had a point, Jack. We've been going round in circles for over a week now and we're still no closer to finding out who actually stabbed Michelle. Supposing we prove Barry Raphael was behind it? It means Paul gets released and put straight on the dole. So much for our gym in Greece.'

'Are you trying to convince me or yourself?' I asked. 'You'll get fifty thousand, but the Raphaels are hardly likely to draw up a written contract to pay the remainder in two or three years' time, are they? We must be treading on some exposed nerves, Tess, to get them making cash offers.'

'She wants to buy you off as well,' Tess added.

'How much?' the businessman inside me asked.

'I think she said ten thousand. She left me her phone number – you're to call her tomorrow morning at ten-thirty. Jack, I've spent the entire evening thinking about the offer and I think I'm going to take her up on it.'

'What about Paul?'

'He'll do two years if it means getting our dream of living in Greece fulfilled. I'll carry on working and saving. I think it's the best way out of this for us. We're ordinary people, Jack, we can't take on the likes of the Raphaels and win. Can you work out how much I owe you and I'll settle up on Monday morning?'

'Yeah. When you going to tell Paul of his conviction?'

'I'm seeing him,' she looked at the white-faced mahogany clock on the wall above the grate, which showed twenty past midnight, 'later this morning.'

'What if he doesn't go along with it?' I asked.

'He will. I'm sure he will. If we don't take the money, Mrs Raphael implied that I would be seeing my name in the Obituary columns of the *Lichfield Mercury*. I'm frightened, Jack. I just want to get out of all this.'

'When did she say she needed your answer?' I asked.

'I've got to phone her tomorrow or today, rather, after I've spoken to Paul.'

'When you get the money, insist on cash,' I said, 'and double-check she doesn't foist you off with funny money.' I got up to leave, and went with Tess to the front door. She engulfed me in her arms.

'Jack, I'll miss you,' she whispered as I moved my hand under her wrap and onto her soft, warm protuberances, encased in panties for once.

'I'll miss you, too,' I said, feeling slightly aroused.

'Goodbye,' she said, pulling away from me and opening the front door. I knew this wasn't her idea of foreplay, so I said, 'See you,' and got into the Allegro. She didn't even watch me go. Twenty minutes later, I was picking Ralph up from outside the Viking.

'You missed one heck of a show, Jack. That Nadine bird was a real goer. At one point she got some old heart-attack case to rub maple syrup all over her body – and I mean *all* over – then she walked into the audience and invited blokes to lick it off. It was like watching a swarm of locusts attack a field of corn.'

'I don't suppose you were slow in getting your tongue out, Ralph,' I said.

'Put it this way – I won't be requiring breakfast in the morning. How did you get on with Tess?'

'Not good. We're off the case. The Raphaels have bought her off.'

'What do you mean, "bought her off"?' Ralph asked. I saw he had maple syrup on his chin.

'She's getting fifty grand to accept Paul's guilt as a foregone conclusion. There's a promise of a further one hundred grand for every year her old man does inside prison. As a bonus, as well, they won't give Tess the starring roll in their snuff movie, either.'

'That's it, then. Back to the grind of serving process and finding fucking mispers,' Ralph said, lapsing into a charcoal-grey mood.

'Apparently Mrs Raphael is going to offer us ten thousand pounds later today in return for our immediate withdrawal from the case.'

Ralph's mood lurched into day-glo yellow. 'That's more like it!' he cried. 'Our first decent pay slip since leaving the police.'

Ralph invited himself over to my place for the night. I wasn't sure whether to make up the bed settee or just tether him to the back door. In any event, he felt the need to finish off the remains of a bottle of Metaxa brandy, puchased on some long-forgotten Greek holiday. I slept with one eye open in case Ralph got the urge to pee in my wardrobe.

At six o'clock I got up and walked down to Chasewater. It had the makings of yet another warm, sunny day. Most of the anglers tended to use the west shore of Chasewater, near the light railway, or over by the retaining wall at the eastern end of the pool. I tried the anglers at the wall first but they were all adults, all prepared for a day's fishing with more provisions than you'd need to climb K2.

I walked through the old amusement park and followed the shoreline. Two teenagers had dug themselves into a little hollow in the shade of a particularly leafy bush. I approached them and introduced myself. They were unable to help but advised me to try a schoolmate of theirs called Matthew who regularly fished from the wall, or the 'dam' as they called it. The dam had been built of furnace clinker and a retaining wall built on top. There's an old pump-house used, years ago, to pump water from the nearby Wyrley and Essington Canal back into the lake. It's hard to believe, now, but a steamboat used to cruise Chasewater which was the local leisure centre for the miners and their families. The lake itself has, over the years, claimed the lives of people who swam less well than they thought they could. The middle of the lake is about thirty feet deep, and the water close to the dam reaches depths of about fifty feet. There is talk amongst the fishermen of a giant pike inhabiting the lake. I didn't care much about the pike. I just wanted to find Matthew.

I saw a kid in a green parka and multi-coloured jogging trousers had set up his nets since I'd last been there. He was sat near the part of the wall daubed with the legend *Fuck Shez*, whoever he was. The kid wore his Nike baseball cap back to front and his trousers tucked into his high-leg trainers. He looked the sort of brat who needed guidance. Preferably to the nearest cliff.

'Matthew?' I asked.

'Who wants to know?' he replied. I detest cheeky kids.

'My name's Jack Mayo. I'm trying to find the two lads who discovered the body of the dead girl here about ten days ago.'

'Are you a copper?' he asked, taking a fish-paste sandwich from his Tupperware box. It was sardine and tomato. I could smell it. They could probably smell it across the lake.

'No, I'm a private detective. Do you know who the kids are?'

'Maybe. What's it worth?' I remember the days when kids would do things for adults without reward, or at least nothing more than an ice cream or two ounces of Maynard's wine gums. Designer footwear and Sonic the Hedgehog put paid to all that.

'A tenner,' I said, trying to keep a tight hold on company finances.

'Make it twenty, mister. A tenner's fuck-all these days.'

I took two ten-pound notes from my pocket and held them up. The kid looked at them and finished chewing a mouthful of sandwich.

'The kids are in my class at school. Jason Mason and Perry Hunt.'

'Jason Mason? Are you taking the mickey?' I said.

'No. His mum and dad were. He lives at number fifteen, Yew Crescent, Chasetown. Perry lives next door, either thirteen or seventeen.'

'How old are they?'

'Fourteen, nearly fifteen.'

'How come they didn't go to the police?' I asked.

' 'Cos they were both wagging school for a start. Then 'cos Jason took her clothes off to look at her tits and that. And he was stupid enough to nick a gold locket she had on. Do I get the twenty quid, mister?'

'Yeah. Where will I find these kids now?' I asked, handing over the money.

'In bed. Neither of them likes getting up before lunchtime.'

'Thanks,' I said, 'tight lines.' ATV's fishing expert Terry Thomas always used to say that. I don't know why I did.

I walked back home and Ralph was just stretching, yawning and farting his way back to consciousness.

'Jack, listen, I've been thinking. Ten thousand pounds buys a lot of naan bread.'

'Go on,' I said.

'But I still think like a cop, Jack. Nobody buys me off –not even for that much dosh. I say fuck the Raphaels. I say we continue the fight to find out who killed Michelle Rosa.'

'I'm glad you think that way. I've just spent twenty quid out of the petty cash, and believe me, Ralph, all our cash is petty, to buy the names of the two kids who found Michelle's body.'

Ralph belched his approval and began to get dressed. Within minutes we were driving to Yew Crescent. Number 15 turned out to be the end house on a block of four council houses. I knew they were council properties because they all had satellite dishes on the upper walls. Number 15 had the added attraction of an overgrown privet fence, peeling paintwork and the wreck of a Ford Escort Mark Two balanced on house-bricks on the front lawn. Ralph knocked on the door. I felt his breath warranted the fixing of odour-eaters to his tongue.

An overweight woman with a nondescript hairstyle and a shapeless, quilted blue nylon housecoat over her shapeless, quilted body, opened the door.

'Yeah?' she said, picking at a slice of soggy toast.

'Mrs Mason? Is your son Jason in?' I asked.

'Who are you? It's half-past bleedin' seven in the morning. He's only been in bed a couple of hours.'

'It's very important. We're private detectives. We need to speak to Jason about the body he found up at Chasewater.'

'What? You'd better come in,' she said, before shouting at the top, or close to the top, of her voice: '*Jason!* Get down these stairs right now. Jason! JASON!'

There was some noise from upstairs before a pale, fat youth with a red spot on his right cheek came downstairs. Ralph said later that the kid's cheek looked like the flag of Japan.

'Jason, these two men are detectives. They want to talk to you,' Mrs Mason said.

She led us into the living room, where a mongrel dog lay asleep on a threadbare rug in front of the gas fire. The house smelt like a dog's leg-pit. This particular mutt looked in the latter stages of its life. Two paws in the grave, perhaps. Presumably it had the same problems as old people and urinated in its sleep. I decided not to stroke it before getting a tetanus booster.

'Would you like a cup of tea, Mr . . . ?' Mrs Mason asked.

'Mayo. This is Ralph Grice, my partner. Not for me, thanks.'

'Me neither, duck,' said Ralph. 'I've got bad wind this morning.'

'Jason, we were given your name by a lad called Matthew who fishes down at Chasewater. He reckons you and your friend Perry Hunt found the body of that woman the other day. Is that right?' I decided not to sit down.

'I don't know what you're talking about,' Jason replied helpfully. He was wearing a Wolverhampton Wanderers football shirt and pyjama trousers.

'I think you know exactly what we're talking about. We're not policemen, Jason, we're private detectives, and you're not in any trouble. Well?' I tried to put fat boy at his ease.

'Me and Perry were down at the pool with our fishing gear. We saw this car parked with its lights off but its door open. When we got close to, we saw the inside light was on and there was a woman in the driver's seat. She was bleeding from her chest.'

'Was she still alive?' Ralph asked.

'Yes. She was mumbling. Perry ran off to call for an ambulance. I stayed with her.'

'What was she saying?' I asked.

'I don't know. It sounded like "again" and "again". Then Perry got back and we scarpered.'

'Why did you run off?' I asked.

' 'Cos we were going to wag school again. We thought we'd get into trouble.'

'Any other reasons?'

Jason hesitated before saying, 'No.'

'Isn't that somebody at your door, Mrs Mason?' Ralph said, and took the mother out of the room. He was ahead of the game.

I was alone with Jason.

'I know you opened her clothes, Jason, and stole a locket from around her neck. Don't worry, I won't tell your mum. Just tell me the truth.' I looked him hard in the eyes. They turned watery.

'She passed out. I was bored, so I undid her blouse. She wasn't wearing a bra. I just looked at her tits, that's all. I didn't take the locket from her neck. It was in her hand.'

'Where is it now?' I asked.

'Upstairs.'

'Go get it, son.' I looked at him with a modest amount of contempt. He ran upstairs and returned, almost immediately, with the gold locket and chain. It was a nine-carat-gold SOS talisman. My heart began to beat faster. My mouth went dry. If this locket was in her hand, then Michelle could have torn it from her killer's neck. The talisman provided details of the owner in case of an emergency.

'Did you open the locket?' I asked.

'No. I just hid it,' fat boy replied.

I looked at the talisman. It resembled something you'd buy from a Bull Ring fly-pitcher. I opened it up and removed the folded, hexagonal-shaped paper from inside. It told me a lot. The owner was born on 28 March 1963. His star sign was Aries the ram, his blood group O (like 47 per cent of the population), and he lived at 38 Upper Hospital Lane, Burntwood, which, if my memory was ticking over properly, was near St Matthew's Hospital. The talisman also told me that Cain Netto, the bodybuilder with hair like Samson, had some explaining to do.

Ralph came back in with Mrs Mason. He was eating a piece of soggy toast and supping the cup of tea he'd earlier turned down. We left after swearing Jason to silence, for the time being, and went back to my house. I made some breakfast and, at ten o'clock precisely, rang Mrs Helen Raphael. I'd swear I could smell her perfume over the phone. She invited me for lunch in Lichfield and to hear her 'little proposition'. We arranged to meet in Beacon Park, at the statue of Captain Smith, the man who went down with the *Titanic*. It seemed strangely apt, in the circumstances.

Ralph dropped me off in Bird Street and I spent ten minutes watching a game of bowls before getting to the statue at noon. I'd worn a light grey suit for the occasion and carried the jacket over my left shoulder. It was uncomfortably hot again and I felt the urge to loosen my tie and unbutton my shirt, but I resisted.

Mrs Raphael was already at the statue. Alone. She wore a two-piece suit in powder blue, with an embroidered design on the collar. The skirt was just below knee length. She'd rolled up the jacket sleeves in a way which was stylish three years ago but rather passé now – a bit like Ralph's sweatshirt which carries the *Birmingham for the* 1992 *Olympics* logo and which he still regularly wears. That was *de rigueur* in '87. The Comic Relief nose on the radiator grille of his Allegro needed looking at, too.

Helen Raphael wore a white chiffon blouse under her fastened jacket. Her perfume followed her like a jet's vapour trail. She did smell good – she had the smell of wealth. She smiled when she saw me and held out her hand. I shook it, hoping she wouldn't notice the sweat on mine.

'Thanks for meeting me, Jack. I've taken the liberty of booking a table for lunch – my treat. No objections, I hope?'

'None at all,' I said. Maybe there is such a thing as a free lunch after all. We walked out of Beacon Park, across the road and along the walk by Minster Pool. The walk was crowded with people looking at the works of art on display and for sale, and people just relaxing or feeding the ducks. Helen admired an oil painting depicting a view of Lichfield in which the Ladies of The Vale featured prominently. I stood behind, admiring a figure in which two shapely tanned legs featured prominently.

We talked of inoffensive things as we strolled through Lichfield's busy streets, topics like the weather or the growing unrest in, yes, Azerbaijan. She seemed reluctant to get to the nitty gritty, and I was reluctant to talk of the proposed offer I knew was forthcoming until after I'd lunched well at her expense. Talking of lunching, we were getting perilously close to McDonald's. I hoped she didn't think I was the sort of guy you could twist round your finger on the strength of a Big Mac and root beer.

My fears were unfounded. She led me round the corner and into a quaint old restaurant called Hector's Place. Mrs Raphael was good enough to advise me that Edmund Hector had been one of Dr Johnson's childhood friends. That accounted for all the Johnson paraphernalia in the olde worlde restaurant. A good-looking young man with blond hair and dressed like one of the Lionel Blair Dancers directed us to a table in the bar area and took our order. Helen ordered a Classic Pimm's. I had a gin and tonic.

On the wall behind Helen was a framed Rowlandson print. Underneath it was a saying from Johnson, something about the morals of a whore. I looked again at the print and saw it was of a guy in a three-cornered hat copping a feel of a busty girl carrying a milk pail. Helen watched me then turned to look at the same picture.

'They were quite bawdy in those days, Jack,' she said, almost shyly. 'Did you know that Boswell used to meet with prostitutes in St James's Park? And he used to copulate on Westminster Bridge.'

'You didn't invite me here, Helen, to discuss Boswell's sex life. What's this all about?' The waiter brought our drinks across and Helen remained silent until he'd done a Donald.

'I went to see Theresa Johnson last night. I want an end to this whole sorry business, Jack. I offered her a substantial sum of money to drop this silly investigation, and she promised to discuss it with her husband. Today, she phoned me to say they'd accept the offer. That just leaves you and your partner.'

A woman who looked like something hideous from the Shadow Cabinet came across and told us our table was ready. We followed her through into a room overlooking the street. Bottle green curtains were draped at the windows. The walls were simply painted in magnolia and adorned with more Rowlandson prints, water colours of old Lichfield and the wit and wisdom of Doc Johnson.

I put my jacket over the back of my seat and sat down at the solid pine table. Helen did the same with her jacket. I couldn't help but notice that she was wearing nothing under her white chiffon blouse. The view from where I sat was terrific. I could almost count the freckles on her chest. She sat with her arms folded in front of her, as if to preserve some modesty. The ugly waitress returned with two impressive menus and a wine list.

'You choose the wine, Jack,' Helen said, hiding her assets behind the menu. I opened the wine list and plumped for a nice Châteauneuf du Pape at a cool fifteen quid a bottle.

'I'll start with the seafood and pasta gratin, followed by the roast pheasant and fresh vegetables,' she said, handing the menu back and folding her arms again.

'I'll start with the button mushrooms in Stilton sauce and then the pheasant as well, please.' I handed our menus to the beast in the French maid's outfit and she waltzed off.

'Where were we? Oh, yeah. You bought off Tess and Paul,

now you're worried about me and Ralph. What's your proposition, Mrs Raphael?'

'A payment, in cash of course, of five thousand pounds.'

'In return for?' I asked.

'Just your silence. Five thousand and you return to your little office in Sparkbrook and forget the Raphaels, or the Johnsons for that matter, ever existed.'

'Five grand,' I said, picking at a freshly-baked bread roll. 'That's a lot of money. Two weeks' pocket money for you, Helen.'

She looked embarrassed to hear that last remark. She unfolded her arms and stretched them out before her on the table. I was suddenly gazing through her diaphanous blouse at her forty-five-year-old breasts. I wasn't disappointed. They were small, but well-shaped and obviously firm. You could have used her nipples as a coat rack. She smiled as I struggled in vain to divert my eyes. Somehow they always seemed to return to her chest.

'Well, Jack. What are your thoughts on the offer?' she asked, as the wine arrived. The waiter poured a small amount into my glass. I sniffed it, swirled it around and then took a mouthful. I told the waiter it was fine and he poured two glasses whilst considering Mrs Raphael's bosom.

'It's not a lot of money split between two, Helen.'

'Do you know how much money Dr Johnson got for writing his dictionary?' she asked, sipping the red wine from a crystal glass.

'No, but I'm sure you'll tell me.'

'Less than sixteen hundred pounds – for a work that took years to complete.'

'I'm not sure I get your point,' I said, still staring at two other points.

'If you continued your investigation, you'd get your lousy fifty pounds a day plus expenses. This way you earn two and a half thousand pounds for doing nothing.'

'It's not much to buy somebody's silence over a murder, though, is it?' I said, as the first course arrived.

The waitress ambled away and I began to digest the mushroom concoction before me. Helen was quiet again. Finally, she spoke.

'Ten thousand, Jack, and not a penny more. That's the best I can do. It's from my money, not my husband's.'

I had the advantage over Mrs Raphael. I knew that Cain Netto had killed Michelle, probably on Barry Raphael's instructions, and that she, Helen, was having an affair with him. She was trying to buy me off to save her lover's skin. I guessed she didn't much care about Barry, apart from the fact that the gravy train might get derailed if he went inside.

'What else?' I said.

'What do you mean?' she asked, narrowing her eyes.

'You're an attractive woman, Helen. Very attractive. I'm sure we could come to some sort of arrangement.' I was pushing her, to see how far she'd go to protect Netto.

She looked down at her food and began playing with it. Then she looked up, smiled, and said, 'You can have me, too, if that's what you want.'

'That's exactly what I want,' I said, reaching across and touching her left breast through the thin white material. 'Now all we need to do is arrange a when and a where.'

I finished my mushrooms and cleaned up the Stilton sauce with a chunk of bread.

'Okay,' I said, using the napkin to wipe around my mouth. 'Book a room at the Chase Hotel in Beacon Street for tonight. I'll see you there at seven o'clock. Bring two attaché cases. One for me containing ten grand; one for Tess containing fifty grand. No forged notes. You got that?'

'Yes. After tonight I don't ever want to see you again. I hardly need tell you what my husband is capable of, Jack.'

The rest of the meal passed in silence and we both declined dessert.

'I'm watching my figure,' Helen said.

'The entire restaurant is watching your figure,' I said, as she called for the bill. She settled up with her Gold AmEx card and gave a ten-pound note as a tip. She put her jacket back on and we left the cool of Hector's Place for the searing heat outside. The wine started to give me a headache.

'Until seven o'clock then, Jack,' Helen said, and she turned and walked off towards Bore Street. I made my way to the bus station and caught a bus to Chasetown.

I began to feel as if Ralph and I were directing things, and that we had control over how this whole business should go now. I went home and Ralph and I discussed our plan to bring the Raphael empire crashing down. We came to a democratic decision, in so much that I told him what we were going to do, and Ralph agreed – after I'd thrown in the six-pack of Ruddles Best Bitter, cooling in my refrigerator.

CHAPTER 11

Ralph and I drove into Lichfield. Specifically, we drove to the Amazon Gym. It was Saturday afternoon and the place was unusually quiet. Ralph still managed to park in such a way, though, as to block in the only other two cars in the car park. I took him inside. A different girl was working on the reception. She had the looks of a young Honor Blackman and the IQ of a gritting lorry.

'Is Mr Netto in today?' I asked politely.

'I'm afraid not,' she said, in the sort of high-pitched whine that could turn any man into an accomplished wife-beater.

'Do you know where he is?'

'Yes, I do,' she said, like it was some sort of a game.

'Watch my lips,' Ralph said in his normal, patient manner. 'Where . . . the . . . fuck . . . is . . . he?' He mouthed the words slowly for her benefit.

'Oh dear, he . . . he's over in Bloxwich at the body-building competition. Or is it Bridgnorth?'

'Listen,' Ralph growled. 'This is VERY important. We need to speak to Cain Netto as a matter of urgency.'

'It's definitely Bridgnorth. That's in Shropshire, isn't it – and it's the Shropshire Open Classic. That's all I know. I only work here part-time on Saturdays.' She was most apologetic. She was most apoplectic, too, it seemed.

'Thanks, miss,' I said.

'Cain will probably be in this evening. Shall I tell him who called?' She was the sort of girl who at thirteen went behind the bike shed to look at somebody's etchings and came out pregnant.

'Yeah. Tell him Destiny called,' I said, opening the door for my grossly-shaped partner.

'I certainly will, Mr Destiny. Bye bye.'

I looked at her sharply for a moment, thinking she was taking the rise out of me, but she wasn't. What a sad indictment of our educational system! Still, we live in an age where kids still leave school with the three 'R's, only nowadays they comprise Robbery, Rape and Riot.

'She's the only person I've ever met with fewer grey cells than Cheapside Police Station,' Ralph opined, as we got in the rusting Austin. 'Now what – Bridgnorth?'

'What time is it?' I mumbled, looking at my imitation Casio. It was three-fifteen. 'I want to nab Netto and get back to Lichfield by seven o'clock ready to meet Helen Raphael.'

'Easy do it,' grunted Ralph, starting up his car and leaving the marked tarmac in a cloud of black smoke.

Ralph guided us to Bridgnorth via the scenic route, through Brownhills, Bloxwich, Wednesfield and lovely Heath Town, Wolverhampton. On the A454 Wolverhampton to Bridgnorth road, we were stuck behind a tractor, which in turn was stuck behind a milk float, which in turn was stuck behind the obligatory old geezer in a checked cap driving his 'X' registered Metro with five thousand miles on the clock. Every road has one. Every traffic jam in the country can be traced back to an old git in a Metro. They're worse than plastic cones. Ralph finally overtook the trio near Hilton and made his usual crude gesture to the Metro driver and his blue-rinsed wife. I think they got the gist of it.

It was four-thirty when we descended through the exposed sandstone high above Bridgnorth. We followed the signs to the town centre, through Low Town, across the River Severn and ascending, steeply, into High Town. Ralph managed to take us the wrong way down a one-way street but refused, then, to give way to the chap in a Barbour jacket driving the Land Rover 'Discovery' covered in horse shit coming towards us. The driver got out and trotted across to Ralph's window. Ralph wound it down.

'I say, old chap, this is a one-way street and you're going in the wrong direction,' the grey-haired driver said in a firm yet friendly manner.

'Can I give you a lift to the hospital, pal?' Ralph snarled.

'I'm not going to the hospital,' the man replied.

'If you don't move that Land Rover you will be.' And my partner gave the man one of his 'looks'. The man complied and we drove on. We spotted a poster hanging from a lamp post advertising the bodybuilding competition at the Sport and Leisure Centre, which we found, more by luck than Ralph's sense of direction, which was Thatcherite at best.

It cost us seven quid each to get inside and the place was packed to the rafters with hard bodies. Ralph's beer gut looked as out of place as a Klansman at a Stylistics concert. Stalls were flogging T-shirts and sweatshirts carrying various gym logos and good old iron-pumping sayings like 'There's no gain without pain' and 'Feel the burn'. Ralph told me he felt the burn all right the morning after a meat balti at Srinegar Mo's. You were nobody here without a shell suit and a suntan. We were nobody.

A guy built like Bridgnorth Castle and with a face which looked as if the J. Arthur Rank Organisation had used it as a gong, took our tickets. It was standing room only in the hall. Over on the stage, a dozen women bodybuilders were going through their well-rehearsed posing routines to the shouts, screams and whistles of the audience. There would not have been enough material in all twelve costumes to have made a midget's scarf.

Ralph stood next to a girl whose face was the colour of Thousand Island Dressing and whose biceps appeared to be on loan from Chuck Norris. She wore those clingy ski pants which had lodged in her various crevices. Ralph studied her curves while I watched the show. The girls bowed and marched off-stage to thunderous applause. I decided you could make a small fortune here as a hair-waxing specialist. Bodybuilders just don't have hairs on their bodies: Action Man has more hair than some of these guys.

There was a temporary lull in the competition while a guest poser from the USA strutted his stuff on the stage. Apparently, he was an ex-Mr Olympia. Needless to say, neither Ralph nor I had heard of him. You could tell he was American 'cos he had white teeth.

The girl in the clingy ski pants moved hastily away from Ralph, and from this I guessed that he had been flexing his own bowel muscles. When the guest poser drifted off, the MC announced the dozen finalists for the 'Mr Shropshire Open Heavyweight Trophy', sponsored by the Bridgnorth *Evening Mail* and Ron's Motor Spares (Salop) Limited. The prize included a cheque for £500, a silver-plated trophy and a subscription to the Bridgnorth *Evening Mail*.

As the MC announced the competitors' names, they bounded onto the stage and froze themselves into a pose. Cain Netto was the fourth one to be called out. He'd tied his long hair back into a pony tail. Ralph doesn't like men with pony tails. 'They belong on schoolgirls and pirates,' he always said.

I nudged Ralph and we left the auditorium and headed backstage. A little jobsworth with a tuxedo two sizes too big or a body two sizes too small tried to stop us getting into the changing area.

'Don't you recognise me, for Christ's sake?' I said, mustering a look of indignity. 'I'm Mr Travis Wicklow.'

The jobsworth looked puzzled but unsure.

'Travis Wicklow of the International Federation of Bodybuilding and Posing,' I said impatiently. 'Oh, show this fool my card, Sebastian, and take a note of his name. I don't want him working at any further bodybuilding events.'

Ralph wasn't pleased to be called Sebastian, I could tell. The name really didn't fit a bloke with a beer gut wearing trousers and brogues.

'Hold on – I recognise you now, Mr Whitlow,' Jobsworth said.

'*Wicklow*,' I corrected.

'Wicklow. 'Course you can go through, sir. I do beg your pardon. Can I bring you a protein drink through?'

'Got any beer?' Ralph grunted, as we walked through to the changing rooms. They weren't clearly marked, and initially we went into the women's changing room. Ruskin would have loved it: the place was like Rubens's studio – not a pubic hair in sight. I took the cup smashing against the wall above my head as a request for us to leave, which we did. We moved down the corridor and stood outside the male changing room. Men with bodies like a Michelangelo statue walked in and out, some just covering their rude bits with towels. I looked at Ralph. I imagined his gut covered his naughty bits. Errol would probably have been here if he hadn't still been engaged in his endurance swim in the Chasetown slurry.

The heavyweights started to come back down the corridor.

'You got your cuffs ready, Ralph?' I asked. He nodded.

Cain Netto got nearly to the door of the dressing room, when: 'Mr Netto,' I said. 'Remember me? I'm the poor bastard you tried to introduce to a lead diet on Thursday night.' And I seized hold of his muscular right arm and right wrist.

'I'm arresting you for the murder of Michelle Rosa,' I

said, and cautioned him. All of a sudden he pulled free, and I was unable to grip his oily arm. His whole body was covered in oil, making him as slippery as a sardine. As Netto ran off down the corridor and out through the crowds, one of his pals tried to block our way. Ralph responded by butting him, then directing his well-aimed brogue at the man's cramped sexual organs.

Netto sprinted out of the Leisure Centre and off towards the High Street, wearing only his cornflower-blue posing pouch, which was just big enough to double as an occasional smoker's tobacco pouch. Ralph and I followed as Netto scattered the shoppers of Bridgnorth along the High Street. Ralph decided to go back and get the car, which was his right in a democracy. I carried on with a stitch in my side, wheezing like an asthmatic. Netto wasn't difficult to keep in view: Bridgnorth isn't the sort of place where you can easily lose a near-naked oily bodybuilder with a pony tail, even on a Saturday. As a matter of fact, it's the sort of place which has strict bylaws to prevent that sort of thing.

Netto pounded across to the driver's door of a red Lada parked near the quaint Town Hall, hauled the middle-aged driver out and jumped in himself. Then he reversed the car out of the parking space and spun the tyres as he headed off towards Low Town. It's not easy to spin the tyres on a Lada. The Russians build them like tanks, and they can be nearly as fast.

At that moment, thankfully, as my knee was throbbing, Ralph drew up alongside me and stopped just long enough for me to get my right buttock on the passenger seat, before accelerating away after our prey. I managed to hang on and eventually pulled the door shut. Netto was heading down West Castle Street with ourselves in hot pursuit. Actually, an Allegro cannot really be considered to be in anything other than lukewarm pursuit. As the Lada screeched around Castle Hill into New Road, Netto failed to notice the Give

Way signs as he approached the blind junction with Underhill, and proceeded to crash into the side of a tractor pulling a cart-load of something rather pungent. It was a smell I knew well from sharing an office with Ralph.

Netto staggered out of the driver's seat of the dented import with blood trickling down his face from a cut on his forehead. He tried to limp away from the scene but the guy in the tractor leapt on him and knocked him to the ground. Ralph and I got to them just before the tractor driver decided to drum the Highway Code into Netto's thick skull with his own thick fist.

'Police. That's enough – we'll take it from here,' I said, holding up my National Trust membership card, and helping Ralph put the handcuffs on Netto. We dragged him back to the Allegro and pushed him onto the back seat.

'What about this mess?' the tractor driver asked.

'If nobody claims it in three weeks, it's yours,' Ralph shouted as we pulled away and headed back to Chasetown. Then: 'Where are we going to take him?' he asked.

'Lichfield Police Station. He's under arrest for murder,' I replied.

Netto, blinking to keep the blood from going in his eye, suddenly regained the use of his tongue, if not his brain. 'You're wasting your time, Mayo. English will have me out before the pubs close.'

'I regret to have to be the one to break the bad news, Cain, but we recovered your SOS talisman, which puts you in the car with the murdered girl at roughly the time she was killed. That's what we call "best evidence" in the prosecution game, Netto me old mucker. We've also got the boy who found Michelle still alive and holding the talisman in her rapidly weakening grip. Things are looking decidedly bleak.' I grinned politely at him.

'I hear there's a refurbished gym at Winson Green Prison, Jack,' Ralph said. 'That's if you don't mind doing a three-man conga with a couple of butch druggies in the showers afterwards. By the time you get out in fifteen years, Cain, you could mistake your back passage for a branch of the Piccadilly Line.'

The look on Netto's face changed rapidly. He gazed out of the car window at the rolling Shropshire countryside, biting his bottom lip, and stayed like that until we reached Wolverhampton's ring road.

'You can't arrest me, Mayo. You're not a copper any more,' he said, with what I detected was a lack of conviction.

'The beauty of the English law is that anybody can make an arrest for murder. And theft. And rape. And lots of other things besides. Makes you feel kind of proud, don't it?' I said.

'What do you want, Mayo?' he asked.

'I got what I want – Michelle's killer,' I said, the grin gone.

'Don't you want to know what happened?' He was pleading now.

'Not me, pal – we have juries for that sort of thing. I'm not a copper any more, remember?'

'Maybe we can do a deal,' he said in despair.

'I'm really not interested, Mr Netto. I'm handing you and the talisman to the police at Lichfield. They might do a deal with you – but I doubt it. The Police and Criminal Evidence Act doesn't really cater for that sort of thing. I think I'm right, Ralph?'

'You're right, Jack,' Ralph confirmed, as we turned off through Heath Town.

We were approaching the Friary roundabout in Lichfield before Netto spoke again. 'For God's sake, Mayo, just listen to what I've got to say, will you?'

'I'm tired of listening, Netto. Three people are dead, and I know you killed at least one of them. The police will listen and they get paid more than me.' I gave him a look of complete indifference, which I'd developed whilst in the CID during countless futile de-briefings.

'I killed Darren Tonks, Mayo,' he confessed.

'Then you're also under arrest for his murder,' I said, in a matter-of-fact sort of way. 'You're a serial killer in the making, Netto. Okay, I'm listening. You've got about two minutes before we pull up outside Lichfield nick. You'd better talk fast.'

'Michelle turned up at Amazon Gym and got a job there. She was good at her work. Then she started an affair with Barry Raphael – which was nothing unusual 'cos he bonks anything of voting age in a skirt. Turns out she's his daughter and he ain't seen or heard of her for over twenty years. She threatened to do him for incest. Eddie English told Barry to play it cool but Barry didn't want the grief of a trial and all the bad publicity, so he paid me to snuff her out. Eddie tried to change his mind but he was wasting his breath. So Eddie planned the whole thing. Paul Johnson was the ideal patsy. He'd started seeing Michelle and Barry wanted rid of him 'cos he was into natural bodybuilding and refused to push the steroids Barry imported.'

We were in Wade Street now.

'Go on,' I said.

'Eddie and I followed Michelle when she took Paul home on the Tuesday night. While they were in his place screwing around, I hid in the back of her car with the knife from Paul's locker. When she came out and drove off I put the knife to her throat and re-directed her to Chasewater. Eddie was close behind in his BMW. Michelle parked near the water's edge. Eddie stayed hidden in Pool Road. I got into the front seat. I had rubber gloves on so I left no prints. Michelle begged for her life but I stabbed her, once, in the chest. Then I heard voices so I took off. I was supposed to rough her up a bit, make it look like a rape, rip her clothes and take her torn panties to dump in Paul's locker. I made it to Eddie's car and told him we'd been disturbed. We drove back to the gym, put the knife in Paul's locker, opened Michelle's locker with a master key and put a pair of her panties into Johnson's locker. If we hadn't been disturbed, Johnson would have been stitched to perfection.'

Ralph parked the car in a bay at the front of Lichfield Police Station.

'What about Darren Tonks?' I asked.

'Michelle mentioned him to Vanessa and said he was her step-brother. Raphael found out and paid me to silence him. He was a weedy little fucker so I just whacked him on the back of his neck and threw him over the balcony, along with his bag of glue. Everything still looked kosher until Johnson's wife hired you.'

'How do the others at the gym fit into all of this?' I felt at liberty to ask.

'Errol was Mr Big when it came to the anabolic steroids; he pushed them like they were Chicken McNuggets. Vanessa and Beverley both took them, so did Barry – even his wife, Helen. Eddie English gathered everyone together and told us that Michelle was dead and that when the police began questioning, we were to make it look like Johnson had a crush on her, but she rejected him. Make it look like Johnson was the bad guy in the whole sorry affair.'

'What about Helen Raphael?' I asked.

'I'm her personal fitness coach,' he said.

'Are you shaggin' her?' Ralph demanded, with a look of despair.

'Yes. Barry Raphael has affairs with anybody he chooses but his wife is forbidden to see other men. She was literally begging me for it. We kept it discreet so she could hold onto her dignity and me to my knee-caps.'

'Did she know about the conspiracy to kill Michelle?'

'Not until afterwards. She helped the cover up when she

found I was involved. I think the silly cow is actually in love with me.'

'It's not mutual, then?' I asked.

'I've been living with Beverley Calvert for over twelve months. When you've got a new Porsche, an old Cortina doesn't excite you any more. Helen showered me with expensive gifts and I was happy to accept them.'

Ralph reversed from the bay and moved off into Frog Lane. 'Where to, Jack?' he asked me.

'Cain's house, first – Burntwood. I think we ought to search your drum, Cain, in case you've got anything else incriminating we can seize. Where are the steroids kept?' I asked.

'There's some at my house, some at Raphael's, a lot at the gym and the bulk of them at Errol's place.'

'You mean the mortuary?' Ralph laughed.

Netto didn't find it very amusing. 'He had a flat in Brownhills,' he said.

I directed Ralph to Netto's home in Upper Hospital Lane. Number 38 was a detached property, probably built in the sixties and probably designed by the same architect who drew up the plans for the Viking pub. It was all roof. Ralph parked on the paved drive, as close to the house as possible. It wouldn't do for the neighbours to see Cain wearing nothing but his posing pouch and a set of Hiatt handcuffs.

'Is anybody likely to be in?' Ralph asked.

'Beverley, possibly. Go round the back and through the gate.'

We followed his instructions and went through the wrought-iron gate into the rear garden. There was a small patio area with a portable barbecue set up, some white, cast-aluminium garden furniture and a green and red parasol advertising Beck's Bier, which Ralph later explained was German for Beck's Beer. Thanks, Ralph. A small breeze-block wall separated the patio from the lawn.

Privacy was maintained with six-feet-high larch-lap fencing on both sides, which was just as well, since Beverley was sunbathing *au naturel* on an old metal-framed lounger.

'Beverley, we have guests,' Cain shouted.

She looked around, and when she saw her man shackled and being led indoors by Ralph and my good self, she came running towards us. It can be a frightening sight, having a naked woman run at you. Ralph studied her form as she approached.

'What's going on?' she cried, apparently oblivious to the fact that she was in her birthday suit. Ralph told me later that he'd like to have tried her suit on, for size. I think I know what he meant.

'I've been arrested for murdering Michelle. Call Barry and Eddie – tell them I need help,' Netto shouted as we began a search of the place. As Beverley picked up the phone in the lounge and began dialling, I grabbed a knife from the kitchen and cut through the phone wire. She wasn't pleased and I found myself grappling with a nude woman. A strong, nude woman, I might add. Failing miserably to put her in any sort of armlock, I resorted to the good old short caution, and Beverley slumped to the floor, out cold.

'Nice touch, Jack,' Ralph commented. 'Why don't you arrest her for decent exposure?'

Instead, I tied her hands behind her back with a tea towel, and began looking around the house.

The box bedroom was the place to be, for in here were dozens of packets of steroids, or what I took to be steroids. Netto subsequently confirmed what they were, even talking us through their uses and side effects.

Ralph picked up a bottle marked Anadrol which contained a hundred 50 mg tablets. Netto told us they were powerful steroids which produced excellent results but had some iffy side effects. He mentioned cancer of the liver, which is a hell of a side effect, just to have a body like

Charles Atlas's. Give me a body like Charles Hawtrey's and a healthy liver, any day. Ralph's liver was probably in a shocking state *without* taking steroids.

Another box contained bottles of methyltestosterone, with the brand name Metandren – 25 mg tablets in batches of a hundred. Netto didn't rate this one. We went through all the boxes and Ralph took a shot at pronouncing some of the names: Oxandrolone, and Aqueous-testosterone suspension, which came in 30 cc vials and which Netto said caused atrophy of the testicles, baldness, acne and infertility.

'People actually buy this shit?' Ralph asked.

'They do. Not only steroids, either. That one there,' Netto said, nodding his head towards another as yet unopened box, 'contains Clenbuterol which bodybuilders and other sportsmen use not to build strength but for increased energy. It means you can continue pumping iron long after the other boys go home. It's actually bovine brain extract.'

'Does that have side effects?' I was curious.

'An increased sex drive, sometimes. All the steroids have harmful side effects of one sort or another. It's just a question of whether the purchaser considers the risk worth taking. Most do.'

'What other side effects?' Ralph asked.

'Headaches, abrupt changes in mood, bitch tits in men, high cholesterol rates, high blood pressure. Need I go on?'

We'd seen enough. Ralph put some samples of each of the various steroids into a box and we took it with us. On the way out I grabbed one of Beverley's garish lipsticks and removed the mirror from the wall above the fire. I wrote on the glass: YOU ARE ALSO UNDER ARREST FOR CONSPIRING TO PERVERT THE COURSE OF JUSTICE and positioned it in front of where she was still dozing. Using some twine from a kitchen drawer, I securely tied her hands at the wrist, discarding the tea towel. I also bound her ankles together. It felt perverted to be tying up a naked woman.

We took Netto back out to the car and drove to my house. Ralph took him inside while I used his car and made tracks for the Chase Hotel in Lichfield.

I parked in a side road off Beacon Street and walked round to the Hotel, which was covered in AA, RAC and *Routiers* symbols, plus the usual Visa, Access, Diners Club and AmEx stickers. I went through the glass-panelled entrance door into the plush, maroon-carpeted foyer. The carpet was nearly as thick as the girl on reception at the Amazon Gym. I approached the desk. It was ten minutes to seven. The young man behind the counter was dressed in grey. Grey trousers, grey shirt, grey waistcoat, grey jacket and navy-blue tie. I guessed his grey tie was in the wash.

'Can I help you, sir?' he asked, in a particularly obsequious manner. He looked like the sort of guy who listed 'cottaging' amongst his hobbies.

'I'm meeting Mrs Raphael here,' I said, in my deepest voice.

'She's upstairs in room ten. She asked me to tell you to go there directly.'

'Thanks,' I said, and he looked down at his work again. I felt the need to get his back up. 'Where do you keep the condom machine in this place?' I asked loudly.

He looked at me like you'd look at one of Bianca Jagger's blouses, and I laughed and ran up the carpeted stairway. Room 10 was on the first floor, the door being situated between a print of one of Canaletto's views of Warwick Castle and a limited edition print by Sir William Russell Flint of several women, inadequately clothed, carrying water jugs around a pool in a courtyard. I knocked on the door, which was opened almost immediately by Helen Raphael.

'Are you alone?' I asked.

'No, I have the City of Birmingham Symphony Orchestra in here,' she smiled. Everyone's a comedian, these days.

I walked inside. The maroon carpet changed to a beige carpet. There was a double brass bed and furniture in antique melamine. Helen had changed her outfit and was wearing an expensive leather blouson jacket in 'taupe', she told me later, but which looked to my eyes like that muddy colour you got at school when you mixed all the poster paints together. It probably came from the same animal which had donated its brain extract to make the Clenbuterol. Helen also wore a matching skirt and shoes and a blouse, probably silk, probably Italian, probably costing if not the earth then several asteroids at least.

'Did you bring the money?' I asked.

She pointed to two matching leather-look attaché cases propped up against the dressing-table leg.

'It's all there, Jack. Every damn penny. Ten thousand in the case to the right, fifty thousand in the other. If you ever show your face again after tonight I'll have my husband eradicate you.'

'He's very good at that sort of thing, isn't he? How many people has he killed? Or, more to the point, how many people has he *had* killed?'

'Let's just finish what we came here for, Jack, and then go. I didn't come here to listen to rhetoric. Help yourself to a drink.' She pointed to the bottle of vodka – Smirnoff Blue Label – on the dressing table. I poured two fingers – two of Ralph's beefy fingers – and sipped it while I checked the contents of the briefcases. They were in order.

'Satisfied?' Helen enquired.

'I hope to be,' I said.

She took the hint and began to disrobe, removing her jacket and placing it neatly on a chair. I looked at her. She had everything money could buy, from designer clothes to fast cars. She was the sort of woman whose farts would smell like lavender.

Helen kicked off her *taupe* high-heeled shoes and unbuttoned her blouse. 'Are you just going to stand there and watch?' she said.

'For the moment,' I said, pouring a second vodka.

Helen removed the blouse and revealed a white lacy brassière. She unzipped the knee-length skirt and calmly stepped out of it. I studied her white, lacy-topped stockings, suspender belt and panties. The white looked good against her tanned skin. She removed her stockings, slowly, like she was beginning to enjoy herself, then she unclipped the suspender belt and twirled it round her head, with a smile. I watched her reach behind her back and unclip her bra. She bent slightly forwards to let her small breasts escape. I could hear her breathing becoming more and more rapid as she tossed the bra aside. Helen looked at me as if for encouragement. I sipped my drink. She slipped her thumbs inside her panties and eased them over her buttocks, then her thighs, before kicking them away. Finally she stood naked, with one hand trying to hide her triangle of light brown pubic hair and the other across her breasts.

'Get on the bed,' I said, 'face upwards.' She did as she was told. 'Now spread-eagle.'

'What?' she asked, looking puzzled.

'Stretch out,' I said. She spread her arms and legs. I took more of Netto's twine from my pocket and tied her right wrist to the right bedpost.

'Jack, I don't do this kinky stuff,' Helen said. I ignored her and tied her left wrist to the other, top bedpost, then her ankles to the two lower brass posts.

'Now are you going to have sex with me, Jack?' she asked, as she was well within her rights to do.

'No,' I said. 'I don't do charity gigs,' and I stuffed a hanky which, frankly, needed washing, into her mouth.

'Here are a few things for you to ponder on as you spend the night here,' I said, collecting up her clothing and grabbing the two attaché cases. 'Firstly, Cain Netto has been arrested for the murder of Michelle Rosa. Secondly, his woman – not you but his *real* woman, Beverley Calvert – is also under arrest. "House arrest" I suppose you'd have to call it, for perverting the course of justice and showing her laundry in public. Thirdly, and perhaps most important of all, I'm now going after your sugar daddy, the immortal, all-powerful, height-restricted bastard Barry Raphael. I'll put the Do Not Disturb sign on the doorknob as I leave. You look like you need a good night's sleep.'

I left the room. I'd have liked to have been a fly on the wall when the cleaner walked in next morning, but the hotel had enough flies on its walls already . . . why add to the problem?

The turd-burglar behind Reception was busy watching his portable black and white TV and didn't see me slipping out. I returned to the car and drove back home, carefully throwing bits of Helen Raphael's clothing out of the window en route. I couldn't help but laugh. I decided I'd even buy my good friend and colleague Ralph Grice a couple or three drinks and a balti, Chasetown-style, to celebrate our success.

Barry Raphael could wait until morning.

CHAPTER 12

I gave Tess a call and invited her along to our little celebration. We met at the Anglesey Arms pub, at the bottom of Chasetown High Street. Ralph and I were on our third pint so we'd probably been there about ten minutes when Tess walked in. She wore a button-through crêpe de Chine dress in coral and cream court shoes. She'd done something to her hair but I wasn't sufficiently knowledgeable to work out what, exactly. You could tell from the movement in her dress that she wasn't wearing a bra. It was Saturday night and the pub was busy. We stood near the bar. Ralph got Tess a Malibu and pineapple.

'I've some good news for you, Tess,' I said.

She didn't say anything, just raised her eyebrows.

'We've got the man who killed Michelle Rosa in custody. We've also got enough proof to put him at the scene of the murder. By the time the forensic boys have been through his house, we'll have him bang to rights. Your husband should be free within a matter of days.' I couldn't hide my satisfaction.

There was no reaction on her face.

'Aren't you pleased?' I asked.

Tess stared at me. A tear formed in the corner of her right eye and I watched it trickle down her cheek.

'Tess, what on earth's wrong?'

'It's Paul, Jack. I went to see him this morning. He looked through me, like I didn't exist.' She began sobbing uncontrollably. I put her head to my chest and led her outside. Ralph finished his pint, ordered another round of drinks, and joined us. We sat at a wooden picnic table outside the pub.

'Tell me about it, love,' I said, trying to sound tender.

'He was like a different person, very negative. He was so down, Jack. I'm scared he'll do something . . . stupid.'

I pulled her closer, as much for my benefit as hers. 'The case is as good as wrapped up,' I whispered. 'Paul will be free within days and you can both get on with your lives. He's bound to be down, Tess.'

Ralph pulled out his hanky. It looked like something you'd tie to the end of a rifle to signal your surrender. I beat him to it and gave Tess a Kleenex.

'Tomorrow morning, Ralph and I are going to lift Barry Raphael. By tomorrow evening you'll be sipping Champagne from Ralph's boots in celebration. It'll all be over. Come on, I'll take you home.'

Ralph hissed in my ear about a balti and I told him it was out of the question. He decided to go alone.

I walked Tess back to my place. Cain Netto was asleep in the spare bedroom with a gag stuffed in his mouth. He was cuffed to the radiator pipe. I took Tess up to my bedroom and told her to get undressed while I made her a milky drink.

When I returned with the Horlicks, she was fast asleep, her dress neatly folded on the floor. I went downstairs and slept on the sofa. Ralph came back later, smelling like downtown Jamshedpur. He began raving about the baltis at the Shalimar. Then he just carried on raving.

I woke at five-thirty on Sunday morning. Ralph was lying on his back on the floor, snoring. At both ends. I woke him by pinching his nose and covering his mouth. I got his attention.

'Time to get up, Ralphie. We're going to call on Mr Raphael. He ain't gonna be pleased to see us,' I said.

Ralph got to his feet and we left the house without even brushing our teeth. The roads were deserted. You could tell it was a Sunday morning from the chip wrappers strewn around the streets by the Saturday night piss-artists. There was a middle-aged guy out jogging in Chase Road. He looked like a sudden death waiting to happen. I wound down the car window to let some breathable air into the car. Ralph needed the toilet, and badly. It was five minutes to six when we arrived at The Old School House and pulled onto the gravel drive. There was no sign of Barry's car.

I knocked hard on the door. No reply. I knocked again: still no reply. We went round the back. The door to the kitchen was locked. There was no sign of life. It was a little early to be catching rays down at the pool but I decided to check anyway. The lawn was covered in dew and an overweight bee was busy snorting pollen from a pretty yellow flower in the well-stocked borders.

Eddie English was down at the pool, but in no position to speak to us. He was floating face down in the water with what appeared to be a bullet wound in the back of his head. His blood had discoloured the turquoise water, as if somebody had let Andy Warhol loose on one of David Hockney's paintings. This was synchronised dying at its best. The position of the entry wound ruled out suicide, unless English was double-jointed. I guessed this was Raphael's idea of severance pay. I walked back to the house while Ralph took a leak in the pool, as a mark of respect.

I smashed the glass in the back door with the handle of a garden rake and opened up. There was no sign of the Filipino housekeeper. What I did find was Helen Raphael sobbing in the lounge. She was sat on the floor, leaning against the couch.

'What are you doing here?' I asked. It seemed a reasonable question in view of the way I'd left her the previous night.

'You dropped my bra in the foyer,' she said, 'and the receptionist checked all the rooms until he found me. You're a bastard, Mayo. Why couldn't you just take the money and go back to your crummy little office?'

Her lip was cut and her face swollen. The ivory satin nightdress she was wearing had been ripped and she held the lacy top up to preserve her modesty, such as it was. There were scratches on her arms and a pearl necklace lay nearby on the floor, with pearls scattered all around.

'Like you,' I said, 'I've got my pride. What happened to you? Barry developing a new love-making technique, is he? Two falls, two submissions or a knock-out to decide the winner? Where is he, by the way? And what the fuck happened to Eddie English?' I gave her these few questions to be going on with, as Ralph joined us.

Helen stood up and the lace gave way to leave her left breast exposed. She hurriedly covered it.

'When I got back here at about four a.m., Barry was arguing with Eddie. Vanessa was here, too. Eddie was trying to persuade Barry to increase his fee, in view of the extra workload involved in stitching Paul Johnson and organising a cover up. Barry doesn't like people putting the arm on him so he took Eddie outside. Five minutes later there was a single gunshot. Then Barry returned and told Vanessa to go and pack her bags. I said, "What about me?" and he began beating me, shouting out that I was a slag, and a dirty fucking whore.'

'So where is he?' I asked.

'He's going to Cyprus,' she said. 'He's got a friend with a villa near Famagusta.'

189

'Fair enough. We'll make our statements to the police, and they can pick him up when he returns.'

'He's not coming back,' she said.

'Then they can extradite him,' I added.

'You just don't get it, do you?' she said, laughing. 'You are even dumber than English thought. Famagusta, Mr Mayo, is in Northern Cyprus – *Turkish* Cyprus – a country not recognised by the United Kingdom after the civil war of 1974. There is NO extradition treaty. Once Barry sets foot there you can kiss him bye bye for ever. He'll live like a king amongst the olive groves.'

'When did he leave?' Ralph asked.

'About fifteen minutes before you got here.'

'Where's he going?' I asked.

'The airport, I suppose. He neglected to mention his itinerary as he beat me, I'm afraid,' she sneered, unaware that her boob was again exposed.

'Which airport? Which airline? Where's he flying to first?'

'Pass on all three,' she laughed hysterically. 'The bastard is finally out of my life. I hope his plane crashes.'

Ralph was busy going through the papers next to the phone. 'Jack – look at this. *Lufthansa: 0855.*' He handed me a slip of notepaper bearing the words and a most intricate doodle.

'You don't mind if I use your phone, do you?' I said, picking up the receiver and dialling directory enquiries. The computer I spoke to gave me the Lufthansa number at Birmingham International Airport. I dialled it and asked the girl if they had a flight leaving today at 08.55 hours.

'Yes,' she replied. 'Flight LH 4550 leaves Birmingham at 08.55 hours for Frankfurt.'

'Ralph, he's flying from Birmingham to Frankfurt at five to nine this morning.' I looked at my watch. Six forty-five.

'Once he's reached Frankfurt, he can get to any place on earth,' Ralph grunted. 'We'd better get a spurt on.'

We ran outside, jumped into Ralph's Allegro and went head-down, mindless boogie towards the airport, only to come to an abrupt halt at the Monterrey Island in Lichfield. The damn piece of junk had run out of petrol! I delivered a few choice words to my partner before getting out and flagging down the first car to approach.

As fate would have it, this was an X Registration Metro in bile green, driven by a chap who looked like Manny Shinwell's dad.

'Police emergency,' I said, holding up my Staffordshire Library card. 'Take us to Birmingham Airport, and step on it.' Ralph and I got into the car, Ralph sitting in the rear.

'Always glad to help the police,' the old chap said, before moving off at a sedate twenty-five miles per hour.

'Does this thing go any faster?' Ralph asked.

'I've had it up to thirty-five,' the old man said, with no little pride in his voice.

'Pull over,' Ralph said. 'I'll drive.'

Shinwell's Pa got in the rear and Ralph tried to get the one-litre Metro to perform like some fuel-injected Jap job. He took the A38 to Bassett's Pole before joining the A446 London Road which took us right through Stonebridge Island on the A45 Birmingham to Coventry Road. The old chap had disappeared somewhere under the back seat when Ralph reached seventy miles an hour.

We turned right, on two wheels, at Stonebridge Island and raced along the A45 towards Birmingham. At Bickenhill roundabout we followed the signs for Birmingham International Airport, negotiated another couple of roundabouts, marvelled at the statue of several pterodactyls called 'Take Off' and headed past the long-stay car parks with rows and rows of shiny cars for Brummie car thieves to screw.

'Euro-Hub or Main Terminal?' Ralph asked, as I read the signposts.

'Euro-Hub for British Airways, all other airlines go to Main Terminal,' I mumbled to myself. 'Main Terminal, Ralph.' He skidded to a halt next to the sign imaginatively called 'Main Avenue' and we got out of the smoking Metro.

'What's your name?' I called to the old man.

'Ernest Brabrook,' he quavered, from the rear footwell.

'There's a Commendation in this for you!' I shouted as we ran towards the brown-tinted glass structure. Ralph took us in the doors marked ARRIVALS, which meant clawing our way through the crowds waiting for Auntie Mabel's return from Mallorca before reaching the huge departure hall.

Several queues of passengers had formed at the check-in desks, inching forwards with their suitcases and just one piece of baggage for the cabin, thank you very much. Ralph kept his eyes peeled for Raphael while I scanned the electronic departure board. FARO ... THESSALONIKI ... COPENHAGEN ... ST HELIER ... PARIS ... FRANKFURT. *Found it!* Flight LH 4550 to Frankfurt, lit up in bright yellow on the black board. It was scheduled for 08.55 hours, the estimated take-off was the same – 08.55 – and passengers were advised to check in at Desks 4 and 5 before going to Lounge A.

'Trust the soddin' Germans to be bang on time,' Ralph commented. It was now seven thirty-five but we still had to locate Raphael. If he'd gone through Customs we'd have to hand it over to the cops and I wanted to nick the son of a bitch myself. Ralph delicately pushed his way to the front of the Lufthansa queue and spoke to the very attractive blonde girl in a red uniform.

'Could you tell me if Mr Raphael has checked in yet, please? He forgot to pack his willy-warmer.'

The girl tapped the details into her computer console and read from the screen. 'Yes. Mr Raphael checked in with Miss V. Lewis. He should have gone to Lounge A now.'

'Thanks,' said Ralph, 'let's have dinner some time.' The girl looked at Ralph in disbelief, before ducking under her desk in an apparent search for a spare Lufthansa sickbag.

We took the escalator to the first-floor waiting area, and began scanning the fast-food establishments, bookstalls and rows of seats for Raphael, but there was no sign of him or Vanessa. Ralph offered to buy me a coffee and we took seats in the Granary. My partner returned with a tray bearing two little stainless steel coffee pots, cups, saucers and plastic pods of UHT milk.

'Ninety-nine pence for a cup of coffee,' Ralph moaned, like he was already regretting offering to pay. 'We can get a jar of coffee for that price.'

'We can get two jars of the shit we drink,' I corrected him.

A tannoy message interruped our meaningful conversation: ATTENTION, PLEASE, ALL PASSENGERS FOR JERSEY AIRWAYS FLIGHT NUMBER JY 2231 TO ST HELIER. WE REGRET TO ANNOUNCE THAT OWING TO TECHNICAL PROBLEMS THE FLIGHT IS NOW SCHEDULED TO DEPART AT 09.30 HOURS. WE APOLOGISE FOR THE DELAY.

Ralph and I watched as happy holidaymakers lounged around waiting for their flights to Spain and Greece and other summer destinations. Many were already wearing their Costa clothing – shorts on painfully white legs, vividly coloured vests, sunglasses, last year's Corfu T-shirt and flip-flops. I experienced a sudden desire to be on a beach somewhere. Anywhere – except Burnham-on-Sea . . .

'Well, Ralph, it looks like we turn it over to the Airport Police. We do the legwork and L Division get the glory,' I said, and began to get up from my seat. As I did so, I noticed the attractive woman looking at the revolving paperback book display at W. H. Smith's. She was wearing a red and white hooped top and tight denim shorts which showed off her tanned, muscular legs. I recognised the shape of her glutes: it was Vanessa Lewis. She had her sunglasses pushed back on her head as she read the blurb on the back of a two-inch thick blockbuster.

'That's Vanessa, at the bookstall, Ralph! Barry Raphael can't be too far away. Let's split up.'

Ralph went over by the entrance to the Mag-Lev transit link to the NEC, while I waited near the entrance to Lounge A. I could still see Vanessa from where I hid. Ralph began using his own semaphore system which he'd never explained to me.

I was studying Vanessa's invisible pantie line when the door to the male toilets to my left opened and Barry Raphael emerged, a big grin on his face, like he'd just fleeced the cleaner out of twenty pence. He was dressed in the sort of multi-coloured T-shirt that looks best on a twelve-year-old, and purple Bermuda shorts. His white Pony basketball boots looked new on this morning. He carried a black leather attaché case in his left hand and a Woolworths plastic carrier in the other. Ralph had spotted the look on my face.

'Hey, Raphael!' I shouted.

He looked across at me and the grin receded like the tide at Weston-Super-Mare. Vanessa dropped the book she was holding. A uniformed cop came into my peripheral vision, over to the left.

Raphael pulled a handgun from the Woolworths bag and aimed it at me. I dived for cover behind a fat guy tucking into pasta in the cafeteria. I heard a shot ring out and the subsequent screams and shouts of the ensuing mass hysteria.

I got up and saw there was a heckler in Raphael's audience. More accurately, it was the Heckler & Koch semi-automatic machine gun with which the uniformed cop had taken aim.

'Armed police. Drop your weapon. Now!' the cop shouted. Raphael couldn't have chosen a worse place to pull his gun.

At that moment, Barry Raphael did something he would regret for the rest of his life – which, as it turned out, was to be less than a minute long. He pointed his .22 pistol at the cop, who fired three rounds into the tanned torso of the would-be fugitive. Raphael flew backwards like he'd been struck amidships by an invisible bull, and landed draped over a well-kept potted plant. His Group AB began leaking from his body like oil from the *Torrey Canyon*. Raphael's death mask would have made a macabre jelly-mould, I thought, as I moved towards his pitiful body in all the confusion. Vanessa also ran to Raphael and tried, in vain, to stop the blood loss.

'I've got a styptic pencil you can borrow, love,' Ralph said – helpfully, I thought.

It wasn't long before the place was crawling with police, and ambulance sirens could be heard in the distance. Ralph somehow managed to melt away – along with Raphael's attaché case. I considered how professional the Firearms cops were these days. When I joined, the Force armoury contained a set of duelling pistols and a rusting blunder-buss. If you called out Firearms to an incident in those days, they'd turn up, shoot a member of the public and piss off for a debriefing in the nearest boozer.

Vanessa was covered in Raphael's blood as she hugged his now lifeless body and called his name, like he was in a position to respond.

Such is life. You spend three hours struggling to put on a bulletproof vest, only to get shot in the arse. Raphael was in poor shape and, to be honest, I was looking at the sort of scene that would make Sam Peckinpah puke. I went for another coffee before I got roped into assisting the police with their enquiries. The fat guy was still eating his pasta like nothing had happened.

At three o'clock that afternoon I was still at the airport

police station crossing the Ts and dotting the Is in my forty-page witness statement. I phoned Ralph, who, it turned out, had caught a taxi back to my place. He arranged for Lichfield Police to collect Cain Netto and Beverley Calvert. Ralph told me he had found a note from my wife stuck to the fridge door with a Rupert the Bear magnet. The gist of it was that she had come home, found a naked woman in her bed, a near-naked bodybuilder cuffed to the central heating in the box bedroom, and had decided to bugger off back to Burnham. Great, I thought.

I made things hard for myself at the cop-shop by refusing to talk to anybody except Detective Sergeant Pillinger. I told the airport police I was his sarbut. Pillinger couldn't detect a gas leak with a naked flame but I thought it was the least I could do. He'd have a nervous breakdown trying to put a committal file together. I told him where Errol could be found – if he hadn't already been discovered – where Eddie English now practised law, and where he could find sufficient anabolic steroids to cater for the Barcelona Olympics. Pillinger had an acute headache by the time I grabbed a taxi home.

My house was empty. Ralph had left a note – ten words, nine spelling mistakes – telling me he'd gone to put petrol in his car. Tess had left a note – fifteen words, one error – telling me she'd gone home. Ralph had given her the case from Helen Raphael containing the fifty thousand pounds. I poured myself a triple scotch, put my feet up and watched the old black and white Cary Grant movie on BBC 1.

Some days later, I found out that Raphael's attaché case had apparently contained about one hundred thousand pounds in used fifty-pound notes. He liked to travel light. Some nimble-fingered git at the airport had scarfed it during the confusion.

You can't even die these days without somebody rifling through your pockets.

EPILOGUE

It's early afternoon on Tuesday 8 December, six months after the Raphael incident. The warmth of the summer sun is long gone as I look out at a depressing dark grey sky, so low you feel you could reach out and touch it.

In September Ralph and I received a postcard marked 'Hellenic Republic', which Ralph claimed was near Greece. Thanks, Ralph. Tess and Paul had moved to Thassos and started putting the murder business behind them. They planned to open a bar in Thassos Town ready for next summer and Ralph and I were given open invites. I remember looking at the picture on the postcard, a place called 'Golden Beach' and how my mind wandered off at a tangent as I imagined Tess strolling naked along the sand.

In November, Cain Netto appeared at Stafford Crown Court where he had the nerve to plead Not Guilty to the murder of Michelle Rosa and Not Guilty to the murder of Darren Tonks. The jury convicted him of the first count and acquitted him of the second. He was sentenced to life imprisonment and I hear he's studying inside to become a lawyer.

Beverley Calvert and Helen Raphael pleaded Guilty to attempting to pervert the course of justice. They were each given a conditional discharge and, probably, a donation from the Poor Box. The Old School House was up for sale when I last drove past in my new Audi.

I never found out what happened to the two goons who tried to toast me alive in my office. The little guy is probably still at large in his boxer shorts. Nor did Tess ever tell me who it was that recommended me to her.

We have a new office now, having decided to move out of the big city. Ralph and I took a lease on a shop premises in Chasetown High Street. My partner likes it here. As he says, there are four pubs within spitting distance – six, if you can spit like a footballer. Ralph's Range Rover is parked outside on the double yellow lines. The pavement isn't wide enough to support his illegal parking.

He's smoking a cigar the size of a U-boat and dropping ash into our fax machine, even as I write. Ralph claims to have found, if not true love, then at least true lust, at last. He's living in the flat above our office with a tall, busty peroxide-blonde girl called Nadine.

Our secretary is in the kitchen making coffee – Jamaican Blue Mountain, none of that chicory shit. Her name is Donna and she used to work in reception at the Amazon Gym which, sadly, closed. Donna's IQ barely stretches into double figures but she fills a camisole top like nobody's business.

My wife finally brought the kids back with her from the temptations of Burnham-On-Sea and we've booked a second honeymoon for next May in Florida. Ralph's generous offer to make it a foursome was attractive but quickly turned down.

On the negative side, we've received word that Mick Raphael is less than tickled pink about Baby Brother's death and has promised each of us the same sort of lifespan as that enjoyed by your average Palermo judge. Rumour has it that he's suing West Midlands Police. Isn't everybody? Watch this space . . .

THE LICHFIELD PRIZE

The Short Caution by Gary Coyne is the winning novel of the 1993 Lichfield Prize. The 1995 Lichfield Prize is the fourth of Lichfield District Council's biennial literary competitions, and the only one to be promoted by a local authority on a national basis. It is promoted by Lichfield District Council

in association with Orion Books

and James Redshaw Ltd Booksellers.

James Redshaw Ltd
Booksellers

Further details and an application form are available from: Lichfield Prize (SC), Lichfield District Council, Tourist Information Centre, Donegal House, Bore Street, Lichfield WS13 6NE. Telephone (0543) 252109.